A PROBLEM IN COMMUNICATION

"I won't talk without a lawyer," Don answered firmly.

"No? I'm sorry. Don, in setting up your interview I budgeted eleven minutes for nonsense. You have used up four already—no; five. When the eleven minutes are gone and you find yourself spitting out teeth, remember that I bore you no malice. Now about this matter of whether or not you will talk; there are several ways of making a man talk and each method has its fans. Drugs, for example—nitrous oxide, scopolamine, sodium pentothal, not to mention some of the new, more subtle and relatively non-toxic developments. Even alcohols have been used with great success by intelligence operatives.

"And there is hypnosis and its many variations. There is also the artificial stimulation of an unbearable need. Finally there is old-fashioned force —pain." The security officer glanced at his watch and added, "Only thirty seconds of nonsense still available, Don. Shall we start?"

"Huh? You used up the time; I've hardly said a word."

"I haven't time to be fair. . . ."

Between Planets

Robert A. Heinlein

A Del Rey Book

BALLANTINE BOOKS • NEW YORK

For SCOTT and KENT

A Del Rey Book
Published by Ballantine Books

A condensed version under the title *Planets in Combat* appeared in three parts in Blue Book Magazine.

ISBN 0-345-26070-8

This edition published by arrangement with Charles Scribner's Sons

Manufactured in the United States of America

First Ballantine Books Edition: February 1978

Cover illustration by Darrell Sweet

CONTENTS

I

New Mexico

"Easy, boy, easy!"

Don Harvey reined in the fat little cow pony. Ordinarily Lazy lived up to his name; today he seemed to want to go places. Don hardly blamed him. It was such a day as comes only to New Mexico, with sky scrubbed clean by a passing shower, the ground already dry but with a piece of rainbow still hanging in the distance. The sky was too blue, the buttes too rosy, and the far reaches too sharp to be quite convincing. Incredible peace hung over the land and with it a breathless expectancy of something wonderful about to happen.

"We've got all day," he cautioned Lazy, "so don't get yourself in a lather. That's a stiff climb ahead." Don was riding alone because he had decked out Lazy in a magnificent Mexican saddle his parents had ordered sent to him for his birthday. It was a beautiful thing, as gaudy with silver as an Indian buck, but it was as out of place at the ranch school he attended as formal clothes at a branding—a point which his parents had not realized. Don was proud of it, but the other boys rode plain stock saddles; they kidded him unmercifully and had turned "Donald James Harvey" into "Don Jaime" when he first appeared with it.

Lazy suddenly shied. Don glanced around, spotted the cause, whipped out his gun, and fired. He then dismounted, throwing the reins forward so that Lazy would stand, and examined his work. In the shadow of a rock a fair-sized snake, seven rattles on its tail, was still twitching. Its head lay by it, burned off. Don decided not to save the rattles; had he pinpointed the head he would have taken it in to show his marksmanship. As it was, he had been forced to slice sidewise with the beam before he got it. If he brought in a snake killed in such a clumsy fashion someone would be sure to ask him why he hadn't used a garden hose.

He let it lie and remounted while talking to Lazy. "Just a no-good old sidewinder," he said reassuringly. "More scared of you than you were of it."

He clucked and they started off. A few hundred yards further on Lazy shied again, not from a snake this time but from an unexpected noise. Don pulled him in and spoke severely. "You bird-brained butterball! When are you going to learn not to jump when the telephone rings?"

Lazy twitched his shoulder muscles and snorted. Don reached for the pommel, removed the phone, and answered. "Mobile 6-J-233309, Don Harvey speaking."

"Mr. Reeves, Don," came back the voice of the headmaster of Ranchito Alegre. "Where are you?"

"Headed up Peddler's Grave Mesa, sir."

"Get home as quickly as you can."

"Uh, what's up, sir?"

"Radiogram from your parents. I'll send the copter out for you if the cook is back—with someone to bring your horse in."

Don hesitated. He didn't want just anybody to ride Lazy, like as not getting him overheated and failing to cool him off. On the other hand a radio from his folks could not help but be important. His parents were on Mars and his mother wrote regularly, every ship—but radiograms, other than Christmas and birthday greetings, were almost unheard of.

"I'll hurry, sir."

"Right!" Mr. Reeves switched off. Don turned Lazy and headed back down the trail. Lazy seemed disappointed and looked back accusingly.

As it turned out, they were only a half mile from the school when the ranch copter spotted them. Don waved it off and took Lazy on in himself. Despite his curiosity he delayed to wipe down the pony and water it before he went in. Mr. Reeves was waiting in his office and motioned for him to come in. He handed Don the message.

It read: DEAR SON, PASSAGE RESERVED FOR YOU VALKYRIE CIRCUM-TERRA TWELVE APRIL LOVE—MOTHER AND DAD.

Don blinked at it, having trouble taking in the simple facts. "But that's right away!"

"Yes. You weren't expecting it?"

Don thought it over. He had halfway expected to go home—if one could call it going home when he had never set foot on Mars—at the end of the school year. If they had arranged his passage for the *Vanderdecken* three months from now . . . "Uh, not exactly. I can't figure out why they would send for me before the end of the term."

Mr. Reeves fitted his finger tips carefully together. "I'd say that it was obvious."

Don looked startled. "You mean? Mr. Reeves, you don't really think there is going to be trouble, do you?"

The headmaster answered gravely, "Don, I'm not a prophet. But it is my guess that your parents are sufficiently worried that they want you out of a potential war zone as quickly as possible."

He was still having trouble readjusting. Wars were something you studied, not something that actually happened. Of course his class in contemporary history had kept track of the current crisis in colonial affairs, but, even so, it had seemed something far away, even for one as widely traveled as himself—a matter for diplomats and politicians, not something real.

"Look, Mr. Reeves, they may be jumpy but I'm not. I'd like to send a radio telling them that I'll be along on the next ship, as soon as school is out."

Mr. Reeves shook his head. "No. I can't let you go against your parents' explicit instructions. In the second place, ah—" The headmaster seemed to have difficulty in choosing his words. "—that is to say, Donald, in the event of war, you might find your position here, shall we call it, uncomfortable?"

A bleak wind seemed to have found its way into the

office. Don felt lonely and older than he should feel. "Why?" he asked gruffly.

Mr. Reeves studied his fingernails. "Are you quite sure where your loyalties lie?" he said slowly.

Don forced himself to think about it. His father had been born on Earth; his mother was a second-generation Venus colonial. But neither planet was truly their home; they had met and married on Luna and had pursued their researches in planetology in many sectors of the solar system. Don himself had been born out in space and his birth certificate, issued by the Federation, had left the question of his nationality open. He could claim dual citizenship by parental derivation. He did not think of himself as a Venus colonial; it had been so long since his family had last visited Venus that the place had grown unreal in his mind. On the other hand he had been eleven years old before he had ever rested his eyes on the lovely hills of Earth.

"I'm a citizen of the System," he said harshly.

"Mmmm—" said the headmaster. "That's a fine phrase and perhaps someday it will mean something. In the meantime, speaking as a friend, I agree with your parents. Mars is likely to be neutral territory; you'll be safe there. Again, speaking as your friend—things may get a little rough here for anyone whose loyalty is not perfectly clear."

"Nobody has any business questioning my loyalty! Under the law, I count as native born!"

The man did not answer. Don burst out, "The whole thing is silly! If the Federation wasn't trying to bleed Venus white there wouldn't be any war talk."

Reeves stood up. "That will be all, Don. I'm not going to argue politics with you."

"It's true! Read Chamberlain's *Theory of Colonial Expansion!*"

Reeves seemed startled. "Where did you lay hands on *that* book? Not in the school library."

Don did not answer. His father had sent it to him but had cautioned him not to let it be seen; it was one of the suppressed books—on Earth, at least. Reeves went on, "Don, have you been dealing with a *booklegger?*"

Don remained silent. "Answer me!"

Presently Reeves took a deep breath and said, "Never mind. Go up to your room and pack. The copter will take you to Albuquerque at one o'clock."

"Yes, sir." He had started to leave when the headmaster called him back.

"Just a moment. In the heat of our, uh, discussion I almost forgot that there was a second message for you."

"Oh?" Don accepted the slip; it said: DEAR SON, BE SURE TO SAY GOODBYE TO UNCLE DUDLEY BEFORE YOU LEAVE—MOTHER.

This second message surprised him in some ways even more than the first; he had trouble realizing that his mother must mean Dr. Dudley Jefferson—a friend of his parents but no relation, and a person of no importance in his own life. But Reeves seemed not to see anything odd in the message, so he stuck it in his Levis and left the room.

Long as he had been earthbound he approached packing with a true spaceman's spirit. He knew that his passage would entitle him to only fifty pounds of free lift; he started discarding right and left. Shortly he had two piles, a very small one on his own bed—indispensable clothing, a few capsules of microfilm, his slide rule, a stylus, and a *vreetha*, a flutelike Martian instrument which he had not played in a long time as his schoolmates had objected. On his roommate's bed was a much larger pile of discards.

He picked up the *vreetha*, tried a couple of runs, and put it on the larger pile. Taking a Martian product to Mars was coal to Newcastle. His roommate, Jack Moreau, came in as he did so. "What in time goes on? Housecleaning?"

"Leaving."

Jack dug a finger into his ear. "I must be getting deaf. I could have sworn you said you were leaving."

"I am." Don stopped and explained, showing Jack the message from his parents.

Jack looked distressed. "I don't like this. Of course I knew this was our last year, but I didn't figure on you jumping the gun. I probably won't sleep without your snores to soothe me. What's the rush?"

"I don't know. I really don't. The Head says that my folks

have war jitters and want to drag their little darling to safety. But that's silly, don't you think? I mean, people are too civilized to go to war today."

Jack did not answer. Don waited, then said sharply, "You agree, don't you? There won't be any war."

Jack answered slowly, "Could be. Or maybe not."

"Oh, come off it!"

His roommate answered, "Want me to help you pack?"

"There isn't anything to pack."

"How about all that stuff?"

"That's yours, if you want it. Pick it over, then call in the others and let them take what they like."

"Huh? Gee, Don, I don't want your stuff. I'll pack it and ship it after you."

"Ever ship anything 'tween planets? It's not worth it."

"Then sell it. Tell you what, we'll hold an auction right after supper."

Don shook his head. "No time. I'm leaving at one o'clock."

"What? You're really blitzing me, kid. I don't like this."

"Can't be helped." He turned back to his sorting.

Several of his friends drifted in to say goodbye. Don himself had not spread the news and he did not suppose that the headmaster would have talked, yet somehow the grapevine had spread the word. He invited them to help themselves to the plunder, subject to Jack's prior claim.

Presently he noticed that none of them asked why he was leaving. It bothered him more than if they had talked about it. He wanted to tell someone, anyone, that it was ridiculous to doubt his loyalty—and anyhow there wasn't going to be a war!

Rupe Salter, a boy from another wing, stuck his head in, looked over the preparations. "Running out, eh? I heard you were and thought I'd check up."

"I'm leaving, if that's what you mean."

"That's what I said. See here, 'Don Jaime,' how about that circus saddle of yours? I'll take it off your hands if the price is right."

"It's not for sale."

"Huh? No horses where you're going. Make me a price."

"It belongs to Jack here."

"And it's still not for sale," Moreau answered promptly.

"Like that, eh? Suit yourself." Salter went on blandly, "Another thing—you willed that nag of yours yet?"

The boys' mounts, with few exceptions, were owned by the school, but it was a cherished and long-standing privilege of a boy graduating to "will" his temporary ownership to a boy of his choice. Don looked up sharply; until that moment he had not thought about Lazy. He realized with sudden grief that he could not take the little fat clown with him—nor had he made any arrangements for his welfare. "The matter is settled," he answered, added to himself: as far as *you* are concerned.

"Who gets him? I could make it worth your while. He's not much of a horse, but I want to get rid of the goat I've had to put up with."

"It's settled."

"Be sensible. I can see the Head and get him anyhow. Willing a horse is a graduating privilege and you're ducking out ahead of time."

"Get out!"

Salter grinned. "Touchy, aren't you? Just like all fog-eaters, too touchy to know what's good for you. Well, you're going to be taught a lesson some day soon."

Don, already on edge, was too angry to trust himself to speak. "Fog-eater," used to describe a man from cloud-wrapped Venus, was merely ragging, no worse than "Limey" or "Yank"—unless the tone of voice and context made it, as now, a deliberate insult. The others looked at him, half expecting action.

Jack got up hastily from the bed and went toward Salter. "Get going, Salty. We're too busy to monkey around with you." Salter looked at Don, then back at Jack, shrugged and said, "I'm too busy to hang around here . . . but not *too* busy, if you have anything in mind."

The noon bell pealed from the mess hall; it broke the tension. Several boys started for the door; Salter moved out with them. Don hung back. Jack said, "Come on—beans!"

"Jack?"

"Yeah?"

"How about you taking over Lazy?"

"Gee, Don! I'd like to accommodate you—but what would I do with Lady Maude?"

"Uh, I guess so. What'll I do?"

"Let me see—" Jack's face brightened. "You know that kid Squinty Morris? The new kid from Manitoba? He hasn't got a permanent yet; he's been taking his rotation with the goats. He'd treat Lazy right; I know, I let him try Maudie once. He's got gentle hands."

Don looked relieved. "Will you fix it for me? And see Mr. Reeves?"

"Huh? You can see him at lunch; come on."

"I'm not going to lunch. I'm not hungry. And I don't much want to talk to the Head about it."

"Why not?"

"Well, I don't know. When he called me in this morning he didn't seem exactly . . . friendly."

"What did he say?"

"It wasn't his words; it was his manner. Maybe I *am* touchy—but I sort of thought he was glad to see me go."

Don expected Jack to object, convince him that he was wrong. Instead he was silent for a moment, then said quietly, "Don't take it too hard, Don. The Head is probably edgy too. You know he's got his orders?"

"Huh? What orders?"

"You knew he was a reserve officer, didn't you? He put in for orders and got 'em, effective at end of term. Mrs. Reeves is taking over the school—for the duration."

Don, already overstrained, felt his head whirling. For the duration? How could anyone say that when there wasn't any such thing? " 'Sfact," Jack went on. "I got it straight from cookie." He paused, then went on, "See here, old son—we're pals, aren't we?"

"Huh? Sure, sure!"

"Then give it to me straight: are you actually going to Mars? Or are you heading for Venus to sign up?"

"Whatever gave you that notion?"

"Skip it, then. Believe me; it wouldn't make any difference between us. My old man says that when it's time to be counted, the important thing is to be man enough to stand up." He looked at Don's face, then went on, "What you

14

do about it is up to you. You know I've got a birthday coming up next month?"

"Huh? Yes, so you have."

"Come then, I'm going to sign up for pilot training. That's why I wanted to know what you planned to do."

"Oh——"

"But it doesn't make any difference—not between us. Anyhow, you're going to Mars."

"Yes. Yes, that's right."

"Good!" Jack glanced at his watch. "I've got to run—or they'll throw my chow to the pigs. Sure you're not coming?"

"Sure."

"See you." He dashed out.

Don stood for a moment, rearranging his ideas. Old Jack must be taking this seriously—giving up Yale for pilot training. But he was wrong—he *had* to be wrong.

Presently he went out to the corral.

Lazy answered his call, then started searching his pockets for sugar. "Sorry, old fellow," he said sadly, "not even a carrot. I forgot." He stood with his face to the horse's cheek and scratched the beast's ears. He talked to it in low tones, explaining as carefully as if Lazy could understand all the difficult words.

"So that's how it is," he concluded. "I've got to go away and they won't let me take you with me." He thought back to the day their association had begun. Lazy had been hardly more than a colt, but Don had been frightened of him. He seemed huge, dangerous, probably carnivorous. He had never seen a horse before coming to Earth; Lazy was the first he had ever seen close up.

Suddenly he choked, could talk no further. He flung his arms around the horse's neck and leaked tears.

Lazy nickered softly, knowing that something was wrong, and tried to nuzzle him. Don raised his head. "Goodbye, boy. Take care of yourself." He turned abruptly and ran toward the dormitories.

II

"Mene, Mene, Tekel, Upharsin"

DANIEL v:25

THE SCHOOL copter dumped him down at the Albuquerque field. He had to hurry to catch his rocket as traffic control had required them to swing wide around Sandia Weapons Center. When he weighed in he ran into another new security wrinkle. "Got a camera in that stuff, son?" the weighmaster had inquired as he passed over his bags.

"No. Why?"

"Because we'll fog your film when we fluoroscope, that's why." Apparently X-ray failed to show any bombs hidden in his underwear; his bags were handed back and he went aboard—the winged-rocket *Santa Fé Trail*, shuttling between the Southwest and New Chicago. Inside, he fastened his safety belts, snuggled down into the cushions, and waited.

At first the noise of the blast-off bothered him more than the pressure. But the noise dopplered away as they passed the speed of sound while the acceleration grew worse; he blacked out.

He came to as the ship went into free flight, arching in a high parabola over the plains. At once he felt great relief no longer to have unbearable weight racking his rib cage, straining his heart, turning his muscles to water—but, before he could enjoy the blessed relief, he was aware of a new sensation; his stomach was trying to crawl up his gullet.

At first he was alarmed, being unable to account for the unexpected and unbearably unpleasant sensation. Then he had a sudden wild suspicion—could it? Oh, no! It *couldn't* be . . . not space sickness, not to *him*. Why, he had been born in free fall; space nausea was for Earth crawlers, groundhogs!

But the suspicion grew to certainty; years of easy living on a planet had worn out his immunity. With secret em-

16

barrassment he conceded that he certainly was acting like a groundhog. It had not occurred to him to ask for an anti-nausea shot before blast-off, though he had walked past the counter plainly marked with a red cross.

Shortly his secret embarrassment became public; he had barely time to get at the plastic container provided for the purpose. Thereafter he felt better, although weak, and listened half-heartedly to the canned description coming out of the loudspeaker of the country over which they were falling. Presently, near Kansas City, the sky turned from black back to purple again, the air foils took hold, and the passengers again felt weight as the rocket continued glider fashion on a long, screaming approach to New Chicago. Don folded his couch into a chair and sat up.

Twenty minutes later, as the field came up to meet them, rocket units in the nose were triggered by radar and the *Santa Fé Trail* braked to a landing. The entire trip had taken less time than the copter jaunt from the school to Alburquerque—something less than an hour for the same route eastward that the covered wagons had made westward in eighty days, with luck. The local rocket landed on a field just outside the city, next door to the enormous field, still slightly radioactive, which was both the main spaceport of the planet and the former site of Old Chicago.

Don hung back and let a Navajo family disembark ahead of him, then followed the squaw out. A movable slideway had crawled out to the ship; he stepped on it and let it carry him into the station. Once inside he was confused by the bustling size of the place, level after level, above and below ground. Gary Station served not merely the *Santa Fé Trail*, the *Route 66*, and other local rockets shuttling to the Southwest; it served a dozen other local lines, as well as ocean hoppers, freight tubes, and space ships operating between Earth and Circum-Terra Station—and thence to Luna, Venus, Mars, and the Jovian moons; it was the spinal cord of a more-than-world-wide empire.

Tuned as he was to the wide and empty New Mexico desert and, before that, to the wider wastes of space Don felt oppressed and irritated by the noisy swarming mass. He felt the loss of dignity that comes from men behaving like ants, even though his feeling was not thought out in words. Still, it had to be faced—he spotted the triple globes of Interplanet Lines and followed glowing arrows to its reservation office.

An uninterested clerk assured him that the office had no record of his reservation in the *Valkyrie*. Patiently Don explained that the reservation had been made from Mars and displayed the radiogram from his parents. Annoyed into activity the clerk finally consented to phone Circum-Terra; the satellite station confirmed the reservation. The clerk signed off and turned back to Don. "Okay, you can pay for it here."

Don had a sinking feeling. "I thought it was already paid for?" He had on him his father's letter-of-credit but it was not enough to cover passage to Mars.

"Huh? They didn't say anything about it being prepaid."

At Don's insistence the clerk again phoned the space station. Yes, the passage was prepaid since it had been placed from the other end; didn't the clerk know his tariff book? Thwarted on all sides, the clerk grudgingly issued Don a ticket to couch 64, Rocket Ship *Glory Road*, lifting from Earth for Circum-Terra at 9:03:57 the following morning. "Got your security clearance?"

"Huh? What's that?"

The clerk appeared to gloat at what was a legitimate opportunity to decline to do business after all. He withdrew the ticket. "Don't you bother to follow the news? Give me your ID."

Reluctantly Don passed over his identity card; the clerk stuck it in a stat machine and handed it back. "Now your thumb prints."

Don impressed them and said, "Is that all? Can I have my ticket?"

" 'Is that all?' he says! Be here about an hour early tomorrow morning. You can pick up your ticket then—provided the I.B.I. says you can."

The clerk turned away. Don, feeling forlorn, did likewise. He did not know quite what to do next. He had told Headmaster Reeves that he would stay overnight at the *Hilton Caravansary*, that being the hotel his family had stopped at years earlier and the only one he knew by name. On the other hand he had to attempt to locate Dr. Jefferson—"Uncle Dudley"—since his mother had made such a point of it. It was still early afternoon; he decided to check his bags and start looking.

Bags disposed of, he found an empty communication booth and looked up the doctor's code, punched it into the machine. The doctor's phone regretted politely that Dr. Jefferson was not at home and requested him to leave a message. He was dictating it when a warm voice interrupted: "I'm at home to you, Donald. Where are you, lad?" The view screen cut in and he found himself looking at the somewhat familiar features of Dr. Dudley Jefferson.

"Oh! I'm at the station, Doctor—Gary Station. I just got in."

"Then grab a cab and come here at once."

"Uh, I don't want to put you to any trouble, Doctor. I called because mother said to say goodbye to you." Privately he had hoped that Dr. Jefferson would be too busy to waste time on him. Much as he disapproved of cities he did not want to spend his last night on Earth exchanging politeness with a family friend; he wanted to stir around and find out just what the modern Babylon did have to offer in the way of diversion. His letter-of-credit was burning a hole in his pocket; he wanted to bleed it a bit.

"No trouble! See you in a few minutes. Meanwhile I'll pick out a fatted calf and butcher it. By the way, did you receive a package from me?" The doctor looked suddenly intent.

"A package? No."

Dr. Jefferson muttered something about the mail service. Don said, "Maybe it will catch up with me. Was it important?"

"Uh, never mind; we'll speak of it later. You left a forwarding address?"

"Yes, sir—the *Caravansary*."

"Well—whip up the horses and see how quickly you can get here. Open sky!"

"And safe grounding, sir." They both switched off. Don left the booth and looked around for a cab stand. The station seemed more jammed than ever, with uniforms much

19

in evidence, not only those of pilots and other ship personnel but military uniforms of many corps—and always the ubiquitous security police. Don fought his way through the crowd, down a ramp, along a slidewalk tunnel, and finally found what he wanted. There was a queue waiting for cabs; he joined it.

Beside the queue was sprawled the big, ungainly saurian form of a Venerian "dragon." When Don progressed in line until he was beside it, he politely whistled a greeting.

The dragon swiveled one fluttering eyestalk in his direction. Strapped to the "chest" of the creature, between its forelegs and immediately below and in reach of its handling tendrils, was a small box, a voder. The tendrils writhed over the keys and the Venerian answered him, via mechanical voder speech, rather than by whistling in his own language. "Greetings to you also, young sir. It is pleasant indeed, among strangers, to hear the sounds one heard in the egg." Don noted with delight that the outlander had a distinctly Cockney accent in the use of his machine.

He whistled his thanks and a hope that the dragon might die pleasantly.

The Venerian thanked him, again with the voder, and added, "Charming as is your accent, will you do me the favor of using your own speech that I may practice it?"

Don suspected that his modulation was so atrocious that the Venerian could hardly understand it; he lapsed at once into human words. "My name is Don Harvey," he replied and whistled once more—but just to give his own Venerian name, "Mist on the Waters"; it had been selected by his mother and he saw nothing funny about it.

Nor did the dragon. He whistled for the first time, naming himself, and added via voder, "I am called 'Sir Isaac Newton.' " Don understood that the Venerian, in so tagging himself, was following the common dragon custom of borrowing as a name of convenience the name of some earthhuman admired by the borrower.

Don wanted to ask "Sir Isaac Newton" if by chance he knew Don's mother's family, but the queue was moving up and the dragon was lying still; he was forced to move along to keep from losing his place in line. The Venerian followed him with one oscillating eye and whistled that he hoped that Don, too, might die pleasantly.

There was an interruption in the flow of autocabs to the stand; a man-operated flatbed truck drew up and let down a ramp. The dragon reared up on six sturdy legs and climbed aboard. Don whistled a farewell—and became suddenly and unpleasantly aware that a security policeman was giving him undivided attention. He was glad to crawl into his autocab and close the cover.

He dialed the address and settled back. The little car lurched forward, climbed a ramp, threaded through a freight tunnel, and mounted an elevator. At first Don tried to keep track of where it was taking him but the tortured convolutions of the ant hill called "New Chicago" would have made a topologist dyspeptic; he gave up. The robot cab seemed to know where it was going and, no doubt, the master machine from which it received its signals knew. Don spent the rest of the trip fretting over the fact that his ticket had not yet been turned over to him, over the unwelcome attention of the security policeman, and, finally, about the package from Dr. Jefferson. The last did not worry him; it simply annoyed him to have mail go astray. He hoped that Mr. Reeves would realize that any mail not forwarded by this afternoon would have to follow him all the way to Mars.

Then he thought about "Sir Isaac." It was nice to run across somebody from home.

Dr. Jefferson's apartment turned out to be far underground in an expensive quarter of the city. Don almost failed to arrive; the cab had paused at the apartment door but when he tried to get out the door would not open. This reminded him that he must first pay the fare shown in the meter—only to discover that he had pulled the bumpkin trick of engaging a robot vehicle without having coins on him to feed the meter. He was sure that the little car, clever as it was, would not even deign to sniff at his letter-of-credit. He was expecting disconsolately to be carted by the machine off to the nearest police station when he was rescued by the appearance of Dr. Jefferson.

The doctor gave him coins to pay the shot and ushered him in. "Think nothing of it, my boy; it happens to me about once a week. The local desk sergeant keeps a drawer full of hard money just to buy me out of hock from our mechanical masters. I pay him off once a quarter, cumshaw additional. Sit down. Sherry?"

"Er, no, thank you, sir."

"Coffee, then. Cream and sugar at your elbow. What do you hear from your parents?"

"Why, the usual things. Both well and working hard and all that." Don looked around him as he spoke. The room was large, comfortable, even luxurious, although books spilling lavishly and untidily over shelves and tables and even chairs masked its true richness. What appeared to be a real fire burned in one corner. Through an open door he could see several more rooms. He made a high, and grossly inadequate, mental estimate of the cost of such an establishment in New Chicago.

Facing them was a view window which should have looked into the bowels of the city; instead it reflected a mountain stream and fir trees. A trout broke water as he watched.

"I'm sure they are working hard," his host answered. "They always do. Your father is attempting to seek out, in one short lifetime, secrets that have been piling up for millions of years. Impossible—but he makes a good stab at it. Son, do you realize that when your father started his career we hadn't even dreamed that the first system empire ever existed?" He added thoughtfully, "If it was the first." He went on, "Now we have felt out the ruins on the floor of two oceans—and tied them in with records from four other planets. Of course your father didn't do it all, or even most of it—but his work has been indispensable. Your father is a great man, Donald—and so is your mother. When I speak of either one I really mean the team. Help yourself to sandwiches."

Don said, "Thank you," and did so, thereby avoiding a direct answer. He was warmly pleased to hear his parents praised but it did not seem to be quite the thing to agree heartily.

But the doctor was capable of carrying on the conversation unassisted. "Of course we may never know all the answers. How was the noblest planet of them all, the home of empire, broken and dispersed into space junk? Your father spent four years in the Asteroid Belt—you were along, weren't you?—and never found a firm answer to that. Was it a paired planet, like Earth-Luna, and broken up by tidal strains? Or was it blown up?"

"Blown up?" Don protested. "But that's theoretically impossible—isn't it?"

Dr. Jefferson brushed it aside. "Everything is theoretically impossible, until it's done. One could write a history of science in reverse by assembling the solemn pronouncements of highest authority about what could not be done and could never happen. Studied any mathematical philosophy, Don? Familiar with infinite universe sheafs and open-ended postulate systems?"

"Uh, I'm afraid not, sir."

"Simple idea and very tempting. The notion that everything is possible—and I mean everything—and everything has happened. *Everything.* One universe in which you accepted that wine and got drunk as a skunk. Another in which the fifth planet never broke up. Another in which atomic power and nuclear weapons are as impossible as our ancestors thought they were. That last one might have its points, for sissies at least. Like me."

He stood up. "Don't eat too many sandwiches. I'm going to take you out to a restaurant where there will be food, among other things . . . and such food as Zeus promised the gods—and failed to deliver."

"I don't want to take up too much of your time, sir." Don was still hoping to get out on the town by himself. He had a dismaying vision of dinner in some stuffy rich man's club, followed by an evening of highfalutin talk. And it *was* his last night on Earth.

"Time? What is time? Each hour ahead is as fresh as was the one we just used. You registered at the *Caravansary?*"

"No, sir, I just checked my bags at the station."

"Good. You'll stay here tonight; we'll send for your luggage later." Dr. Jefferson's manner changed slightly. "But your mail was to be sent to the hotel?"

"That's right."

Don was surprised to see that Dr. Jefferson looked distinctly worried. "Well, we'll check into that later. That package I sent to you—would it be forwarded promptly?"

"I really don't know, sir. Ordinarily the mail comes in twice a day. If it came in after I left, it would ordinarily wait over until morning. But if the headmaster thought about it, he might have it sent into town special so that I would get it before up-ship tomorrow morning."

"Mean to say there isn't a tube into the school?"

"No, sir, the cook brings in the morning mail when he shops and the afternoon mail is chuted in by the Roswell copter bus."

"A desert island! Well . . . we'll check around midnight. If it hasn't arrived then—never mind." Nevertheless he seemed perturbed and hardly spoke during their ride to dinner.

The restaurant was misnamed *The Back Room* and there was no sign out to indicate its location; it was simply one of many doors in a side tunnel. Nevertheless many people seemed to know where it was and to be anxious to get in, only to be thwarted by a stern-faced dignitary guarding a velvet rope. This ambassador recognized Dr. Jefferson and sent for the *maître d'hôtel*. The doctor made a gesture understood by headwaiters throughout history, the rope was dropped, and they were conducted in royal progress to a ringside table. Don was bug-eyed at the size of the bribe. Thus he was ready with the proper facial expression when he caught sight of their waitress.

His reaction to her was simple; she was, it seemed to him, the most beautiful sight he had ever seen, both in person and in costume. Dr. Jefferson caught his expression and chuckled. "Don't use up your enthusiasm, son. The ones we have paid to see will be out there." He waved at the floor. "Cocktail first?"

Don said that he didn't believe so, thank you.

"Suit yourself. You are man high and a single taste of the fleshpots wouldn't do you any permanent harm. But suppose you let me order dinner for us?" Don agreed. While

Dr. Jefferson was consulting with the captive princess over the menu, Don looked around. The room simulated outdoors in the late evening; stars were just appearing overhead. A high brick wall ran around the room, hiding the non-existent middle distance and patching in the floor to the false sky. Apple trees hung over the wall and stirred in the breeze. An old-fashioned well with a well sweep stood beyond the tables on the far side of the room; Don saw another "captive princess" go to it, operate the sweep, and remove a silver pail containing a wrapped bottle.

At the ringside opposite them a table had been removed to make room for a large transparent plastic capsule on wheels. Don had never seen one but he recognized its function; it was a Martian's "perambulator," a portable air-conditioning unit to provide the rare, cold air necessary to a Martian aborigine. The occupant could be seen dimly, his frail body supported by a metal articulated servo framework to assist him in coping with the robust gravity of the third planet. His pseudo wings drooped sadly and he did not move. Don felt sorry for him.

As a youngster he had met Martians on Luna, but Luna's feeble field was less than that of Mars; it did not turn them into cripples, paralyzed by a gravity field too painful for their evolutionary pattern. It was both difficult and dangerous for a Martian to risk coming to Earth; Don wondered what had induced this one. A diplomatic mission, perhaps?

Dr. Jefferson dismissed the waitress, looked up and noticed him staring at the Martian. Don said, "I was just wondering why he would come here. Not to eat, surely."

"Probably wants to watch the animals feeding. That's part of my own reason, Don. Take a good look around you; you'll never see the like again."

"No, I guess not—not on Mars."

"That's not what I mean. Sodom and Gomorrah, lad—rotten at the core and skidding toward the pit. '—these our actors, as I foretold you . . . are melted into air—' and so forth. Perhaps even 'the great globe itself.' I talk too much. Enjoy it; it won't last long."

Don looked puzzled. "Dr. Jefferson, do you *like* living here?"

"Me? I'm as decadent as the city I infest; it's my natural element. But that doesn't keep me from telling a hawk from a handsaw."

The orchestra, which had been playing softly from nowhere in particular, stopped suddenly and the sound system announced "News flash!" At the same time the darkening sky overhead turned black and lighted letters started marching across it. The voice over the sound system read aloud the words streaming across the ceiling: BERMUDA: OFFICIAL: THE DEPARTMENT OF COLONIAL AFFAIRS HAS JUST ANNOUNCED THAT THE PROVISIONAL COMMITTEE OF THE VENUS COLONIES HAS REJECTED OUR NOTE. A SOURCE CLOSE TO THE FEDERATION CHAIRMAN SAYS THAT THIS IS AN EXPECTED DEVELOPMENT AND NO CAUSE FOR ALARM.

The lights went up and the music resumed. Dr. Jefferson's lips were stretched back in a mirthless grin. "How appropriate!" he commented. "How timely! The handwriting on the wall."

Don started to blurt out a comment, but was distracted by the start of the show. The stage floor by them had sunk out of sight, unnoticed, during the news flash. Now from the pit thus created came a drifting, floating cloud lighted from within with purple and flame and rose. The cloud melted away and Don could see that the stage was back in place and peopled with dancers. There was a mountain in the stage background.

Dr. Jefferson had been right; the ones worth staring at were on the stage, not serving the tables. Don's attention was so taken that he did not notice that food had been placed in front of him. His host touched his elbow. "Eat something, before you faint."

"Huh? Oh, yes, sir!" He did so, busily and with good appetite but with his eyes on the entertainers. There was one man in the cast, portraying Tannhäuser, but Don did not know and did not care whom he represented; he noticed him only when he got in the way. Similarly, he had finished two thirds of what was placed before him without noticing what he was eating.

Dr. Jefferson said, "Like it?"

Don did a double-take and realized that the doctor was speaking of food, not of the dancers. "Oh, yes! It's awfully good." He examined his plate. "But what is it?"

"Don't you recognize it? Baked baby gregarian."

It took a couple of seconds for Don to place in his mind just what a gregarian was. As a small child he had seen hundreds of the little satyr-like bipeds—*faunas gregariaus veneris Smythii*—but he did not at first associate the common commercial name with the friendly, silly creatures he and his playmates, along with all other Venus colonials, had always called "move-overs" because of their chronic habit of crowding up against one, shouldering, nuzzling, sitting on one's feet, and in other ways displaying their insatiable appetite for physical affection.

Eat a baby move-over? He felt like a cannibal and for the second time in one day started to behave like a groundhog in space. He gulped and controlled himself but could not touch another bite.

He looked back at the stage. Venusberg disappeared, giving way to a tired-eyed man who kept up a rapid fire of jokes while juggling flaming torches. Don was not amused; he let his gaze wander around the room. Three tables away a man met his eyes, then looked casually away. Don thought about it, then looked the man over carefully and decided that he recognized him. "Dr. Jefferson?"

"Yes, Don?"

"Do you happen to know a Venus dragon who calls himself 'Sir Isaac Newton'?" Don added the whistled version of the Venerian's true name.

"Don't!" the older man said sharply.

"Don't what?"

"Don't advertise your background unnecessarily, not at this time. Why do you ask about this, uh, 'Sir Isaac Newton'?" He kept his voice low with his lips barely moving.

Donald told him about the casual meeting at Gary Station. "When I got through I was dead sure that a security cop was watching me. And now that same man is sitting over there, only now he's not in uniform."

"Are you sure?"

"I think I'm sure."

"Mmm . . . you might be mistaken. Or he might simply be here in his off hours—though a security policeman should not be, not on his pay. See here—pay no further attention to him and don't speak of him again. And don't speak of that dragon, nor of anything else Venerian. Just appear to be having a good time. But pay careful attention to anything I say."

Don tried to carry out the instructions, but it was hard to keep his mind on gayety. Even when the dancers reappeared he felt himself wanting to turn and stare at the man who had dampened the party. The plate of baked gregarian was removed and Dr. Jefferson ordered something for him called a "Mount Etna." It was actually shaped like a volcano and a plume of steam came out of the tip. He dipped a spoon into it, found that it was fire and ice, assaulting his palate with conflicting sensations. He wondered how anyone could eat it. Out of politeness he cautiously tried another bite. Presently he found that he had eaten all of it and was sorry there was not more.

At the break in the stage acts Don tried to ask Dr. Jefferson what he really thought about the war scare. The doctor firmly turned the talk around to his parents' work and branched out to the past and future of the System. "Don't fret yourself about the present, son. Troubles, merely troubles—necessary preliminaries to the consolidation of the System. In five hundred years the historians will hardly notice it. There will be the Second Empire—six planets by then." .

"Six? You don't honestly think we'll ever be able to do anything with Jupiter and Saturn? Oh—you mean the Jovian moons."

"No, I mean six primary planets. We'll move Pluto and Neptune in close by the fire and we'll drag Mercury back and let it cool off."

The idea of moving planets startled Don. It sounded wildly impossible, but he let it rest, since his host was a man who maintained that everything and anything was possible. "The race needs a lot of room," Dr. Jefferson went on. "After all, Mars and Venus have their own intelligent races; we can't crowd them much more without genocide—and it's not dead certain which way the genocide would work, even with the Martians. But the reconstruction of this system is just engineering—nothing to what else we'll do. Half a millennium from now there will be more Earth-humans outside this system than in it; we'll be swarming around every G-type star in this neighborhood. Do you know what I would do if I were your age, Don? I'd get me a berth in the *Pathfinder.*"

Don nodded. "I'd like that." The *Pathfinder,* star ship intended for a one-way trip, had been building on, and near, Luna since before he was born. Soon she would go. All or nearly all of Don's generation had at least dreamed about leaving with her.

"Of course," added his host, "you would have to have a bride." He pointed to the stage which was again filling. "Take that blonde down there. She's a likely looking lassie—healthy at least."

Don smiled and felt worldly. "She might not hanker after pioneering. She looks happy as she is."

"Can't tell till you ask her. Here." Dr. Jefferson summoned the *maître d'hôtel;* money changed hands. Presently the blonde came to their table but did not sit down. She was a tom-tom singer and she proceeded to boom into Don's ears, with the help of the orchestra, sentiments that would have embarrassed him even if expressed privately. He ceased to feel worldly, felt quite warm in the face instead and confirmed his resolution not to take this female to the stars. Nevertheless he enjoyed it.

The stage was just clearing when the lights blinked once and the sound system again brayed forth: "Space raid warning! Space raid warning!" All lights went out.

III

Hunted

FOR AN infinitely long moment there was utter blackness and silence without even the muted whir of the blowers. Then a tiny light appeared in the middle of the stage, illuminating the features of the starring comic. He drawled in an intentionally ridiculous nasal voice, "The next sound you hear will be . . . The Tromp of Doom!" He giggled and went on briskly, "Just sit quiet, folks, and hang on to your money—some of the help are relatives of the management. This is just a drill. Anyhow, we have a hundred feet of concrete overhead—and a durn sight thicker mortgage. Now, to get you into the mood for the next act—which is mine—the next round of drinks is on the house." He leaned forward and called out, "Gertie! Drag up that stuff we couldn't unload New Year's Eve."

Don felt the tension ease around the room and he himself relaxed. He was doubly startled when a hand closed around his wrist. "*Quiet!*" whispered Dr. Jefferson into his ear.

Don let himself be led away in the darkness. The doctor apparently knew, or remembered, the layout; they got out of the room without bumping into tables and with only one unimportant brush with someone in the dark. They seemed to be going down a long hall, black as the inside of coal, then turned a corner and stopped.

"But you can't go out, sir," Don heard a voice say. Dr. Jefferson spoke quietly, his words too low to catch. Something rustled; they moved forward again, through a doorway, and turned left.

They proceeded along this tunnel—Don felt sure that it was the public tunnel just outside the restaurant though it seemed to have turned ninety degrees in the dark. Dr. Jefferson still dragged him along by the wrist without speaking. They turned again and went down steps.

There were other people about, though not many. Once

someone grabbed Don in the dark; he struck out wildly, smashed his fist into something flabby and heard a muffled grunt. The doctor merely pulled him along the faster.

The doctor stopped at last, seemed to be feeling around in the dark. There came a feminine squeal out of the blackness. The doctor drew back hastily and moved on a few feet, stopped again. "Here," he said at last. "Climb in." He pulled Don forward and placed his hand on something; Don felt around and decided that it was a parked autocab, its top open. He climbed in and Dr. Jefferson got in behind, closing the top after him. "Now we can talk," he said calmly. "Someone beat us to that first one. But we can't go anywhere until the power comes on again."

Don was suddenly aware that he was shaking with excitement. When he could trust himself to speak he said, "Doctor—is this actually an attack?"

"I doubt it mightily," the man answered. "It's almost certainly a drill—I hope. But it gave us just the opportunity that I had been looking for to get away quietly."

Don chewed this over. Jefferson went on, "What are you fretting about? The check? I have an account there."

It had not occurred to Don that they were walking out on the check. He said so and added, "You mean that security policeman I thought I recognized?"

"Unfortunately."

"But— I think I must have made a mistake. Oh, it looked like the same man, all right, but I don't see how it would have been humanly possible for him to have followed me even if he popped into the next cab. I distinctly remember that at least once my cab was the only cab on an elevator. That tears it. If it was the same cop, it was an accident; he wasn't looking for me."

"Perhaps he was looking for me."

"Huh?"

"Never mind. As to following you—Don, do you know how these autocabs work?"

"Well—in general."

"If that security cop wanted to tail you, he would not get into the next cab. He would call in and report the number of your cab. That number would be monitored in the control-net board at once. Unless you reached your destination before the monitoring started, they would read the code of your destination right out of the machine. Whereupon another security officer would be watching for your arrival. It carries on from there. When I rang for an autocab my circuit would already be monitored, and the cab that answered the ring likewise. Consequently the first cop is already seated at a table in *The Back Room* before we arrive. That was their one slip, using a man you had seen— but we can forgive that as they are overworked at present!"

"But why would they want *me*? Even if they think I'm uh, disloyal, I'm not that important."

Dr. Jefferson hesitated, then said, "Don, I don't know how long we will be able to talk. We can talk freely for the moment because they are just as limited by the power shutdown as we are. But once the power comes on we can no longer talk and I have a good deal to say. We can't talk, even here, after the power comes on."

"Why not?"

"The public isn't supposed to know, but each of these cabs has a microphone in it. The control frequency for the cab itself can carry speech modulation without interfering with the operation of the vehicle. So we are not safe once power is restored. Yes, I know; it's a shameful set up. I didn't dare talk in the restaurant, even with the orchestra playing. They could have had a shotgun mike trained on us.

"Now, listen carefully. We must locate that package I mailed to you—we *must*. I want you to deliver it to your father . . . or rather, what's in it. Point number two: you *must* catch that shuttle rocket tomorrow morning, even if the heavens fall. Point number three: you won't stay with me tonight, after all. I'm sorry but I think it is best so. Number four: when the power comes on, we will ride around for a while, talking of nothing in particular and never mentioning names. Presently I will see to it that we end up near a public common booth and you will call the *Caravansary*. If the package is there, you will leave me, go back to the Station, get your bags, then go to the hotel, register and pick up your mail. Tomorrow morning you will get your ship and leave. Don't call me. Do you understand all that?"

"Uh, I think so, sir." Don waited, then blurted out, "But why? Maybe I'm talking out of turn, but it seems to me I ought to know why we are doing this."

"What do you want to know?"

"Well . . . what's in the package?"

"You will see. You can open it, examine it, and decide for yourself. If you decide not to deliver it, that's your privilege. As for the rest—what are your political convictions, Don?"

"Why . . . that's rather hard to say, sir."

"Mmmm—mine weren't too clear at your age either. Let's put it this way: would you be willing to string along with your parents for the time being? Until you form your own?"

"Why, of course!"

"Did it seem a bit odd to you that your mother insisted that you look me up? Don't be shy—I know that a young fellow arriving in the big town doesn't look up semi-strangers through choice. Now—she must have considered it important for you to see me. Eh?"

"I guess she must have."

"Will you let it stand at that? What you don't know, you can't tell—and can't get you into trouble."

Don thought it over. The doctor's words seemed to make sense, yet it went mightily against the grain to be asked to do something mysterious without knowing all the whys and wherefors. On the other hand, had he simply received the package, he undoubtedly would have delivered it to his father without thinking much about it.

He was about to ask further questions when the lights came on and the little car started to purr. Dr. Jefferson said, "Here we go!" leaned over the board and quickly dialed a destination. The autocab moved forward. Don started to speak but the doctor shook his head.

The car threaded its way through several tunnels, down a ramp and stopped in a large underground square. Dr. Jefferson paid it off and led Don through the square and to a passenger elevator. The square was jammed and one could sense the crowd's frenetic mood resulting from the space raid alarm. They had to shove their way through a mass of people gathered around a public telescreen in the center of the square. Don was glad to get on the elevator, even though it too was packed.

Dr. Jefferson's immediate destination was another cab stand in a square several levels higher. They got into a cab and moved away; this one they rode for several minutes, then changed cabs again. Don was completely confused and could not have told whether they were north, south, high, low, east, or west. The doctor glanced at his watch as they left the last autocab and said, "We've killed enough time. Here." He indicated a communication booth near them.

Don went in and phoned the *Carvansary*. Was there any mail being held for him? No, there was not. He explained that he was not registered at the hotel; the clerk looked again. No—sorry, sir.

Don came out and told Dr. Jefferson. The doctor chewed his lip. "Son, I've made a bad error in judgment." He glanced around; there was no one near them. "And I've wasted time."

"Can I help, sir?"

"Eh? Yes, I think you can—I'm sure you can." He paused to think. "We'll go back to my apartment. We must. But we won't stay there. We'll find some other hotel—not the *Caravansary*—and I'm afraid we must work all night. Are you up to it?"

"Oh, certainly!"

"I've some 'borrowed-time' pills; they'll help. See here, Don, whatever happens, you are to catch that ship tomorrow. Understand?"

Don agreed. He intended to catch the ship in any case and could not conceive of a reason for missing it. Privately he was beginning to wonder if Dr. Jefferson were quite right in his head.

"Good. We'll walk; it's not far."

A half mile of tunnels and a descent by elevator got them there. As they turned into the tunnel in which the doctor's apartment was located, he glanced up and down it; it was empty. They crossed rapidly and the doctor let them in. Two strange men were seated in the living room.

34

Dr. Jefferson glanced at them, said, "Good evening, gentlemen," and turned back to his guest. "Good night, Don. It's been very pleasant seeing you and be sure to remember me to your parents." He grasped Don's hand and firmly urged him out the door.

The two men stood up. One of them said, "It took you a long time to get home, Doctor."

"I'd forgotten the appointment, gentlemen. Now, goodbye, Don—*I don't want you to be late.*"

The last remark was accompanied by increased pressure on Don's hand. He answered, "Uh—good night, Doctor. And thanks."

He turned to leave, but the man who had spoken moved quickly between him and the door. "Just a moment, please."

Dr. Jefferson answered, "Really, gentlemen, there is no reason to delay this boy. Let him go along so that we may get down to our business."

The man did not answer directly but called out, "Elkins! King!" Two more men appeared from a back room of the apartment. The man who seemed to be in charge said to them, "Take the youngster back to the bedroom. Close the door."

"Come along, buddy."

Don, who had been keeping his mouth shut and trying to sort out the confusing new developments, got angry. He had more than a suspicion that these men were security police even though they were not in uniform—but he had been brought up to believe that honest citizens had nothing to fear. "Wait a minute!" he protested. "I'm not going any place. What's the idea?"

The man who had told him to come along moved closer and took his arm. Don shook it off. The leader stopped any further action by his men with a very slight gesture. "Don Harvey——"

"Huh? Yes?"

"I could give you a number of answers to that. One of them is this—" He displayed a badge in the palm of his hand. "—but that might be faked. Or, if I cared to take time, I could satisfy you with stamped pieces of paper, all proper and legalistic and signed with important names." Don noticed that his voice was gentle and cultured.

"But it happens that I am tired and in a hurry and don't want to be bothered playing word games with young punks. So let it stand that there are four of us all armed. So—will you go quietly, or would you rather be slapped around a bit and dragged?"

Don was about to answer with school-game bravado; Dr. Jefferson cut in. "Do as they ask you, Donald!"

He closed his mouth and followed the subordinate on back. The man led him into the bedroom and closed the door. "Sit down," he said pleasantly. Don did not move. His guard came up, placed a palm against his chest and pushed. Don sat down.

The man touched a button at the bed's control panel, causing it to lift to the reading position, then lay down. He appeared to go to sleep, but every time Don looked at him the man's eyes met his. Don strained his ears, trying to hear what was going on in the front room, but he need not have bothered; the room, being a sleeping room, was fully soundproof.

So he sat there and fidgeted, trying to make sense out of preposterous things that had happened to him. He recalled almost with unbelief that it had been only this morning that Lazy and he had started out to climb Peddler's Grave. He wondered what Lazy was doing now and whether the greedy little rascal missed him.

Probably not, he admitted mournfully.

He slid a glance at the guard, while wondering whether or not, if he gathered himself together, drawing his feet as far under him as he could——

The guard shook his head. "Don't do it," he advised.

"Don't to what?"

"Don't try to jump me. You might hurry me and then you might get hurt—bad." The man appeared to go back to sleep.

Don slumped into apathy. Even if he did manage to jump this one, slug him maybe, there were three more out front. And suppose he got away from them? A strange city, where *they* had everything organized, everything under control—where would he run *to*?

Once he had come across the stable cat playing with a mouse. He had watched for a moment, fascinated even though his sympathies were with the mouse, before he had stepped forward and put the poor beastie out of its misery. The cat had never once let the mouse scamper further than pounce range. Now he was the mouse——

"Up you come!"

Don jumped to his feet, startled and having trouble placing himself. "I wish I had your easy conscience," the guard said admiringly. "It's a real gift to be able to catch forty winks any time. Come on; the boss wants you."

Don preceded him back into the living room; there was no one there but the mate of the man who had guarded him. Don turned and said, "Where is Dr. Jefferson?"

"Never mind," his guard replied. "The lieutenant hates to be kept waiting." He started on out the door.

Don hung back. The second guard casually took him by the arm; he felt a stabbing pain clear to his shoulder and went along.

Outside they had a manually-operated car larger than the robot cabs. The second guard slipped into the driver's seat; the other urged Don into the passenger compartment. There he sat down and started to turn—and found that he could not. He was unable even to raise his hands. Any attempt to move, to do anything other than sit and breathe, felt like struggling against the weight of too many blankets. "Take it easy," the guard advised. "You can pull a ligament fighting that field. And it does not do any good."

Don had to prove to himself that the man was right. Whatever the invisible bonds were, the harder he strained against them the tighter they bound him. On the other hand when he relaxed and rested he could not even feel them. "Where are you taking me?" he demanded.

"Don't you know? The city I.B.I. office, of course."

"What for? I haven't done anything!"

"In that case, you won't have to stay long."

The car pulled up inside a large garaging room; the

three got out and waited in front of a door; Don had a feeling that they were being looked over. Shortly the door opened; they went inside.

The place had the odor of bureaucracy. They went down a long corridor past endless offices filled with clerks, desks, transtypers, filing machines, whirring card sorters. A lift bounced them to another level; they went on through more corridors and stopped at an office door. "Inside," said the first guard. Don went in; the door slid shut behind him with the guards outside.

"Sit down, Don." It was the leader of the group of four, now in the uniform of security officer and seated at a horseshoe desk.

Don said, "Where is Dr. Jefferson? What did you do with him?"

"Sit down, I said." Don did not move; the lieutenant went on, "Why make it hard for yourself? You know where you are; you know that I could have you restrained in any way that suited me—some of them quite unpleasant. Will you sit down, please, and save us both trouble?"

Don sat down and immediately said, "I want to see a lawyer."

The lieutenant shook his head slowly, looking like a tired and gentle school teacher. "Young fellow, you've been reading too many romantic novels. Now if you had studied the dynamics of history instead, you would realize that the logic of legalism alternates with the logic of force in a pattern dependent on the characteristics of the culture. Each culture evokes its own basic logic. You follow me?"

Don hesitated; the other went on, "No matter. The point is, your request for a lawyer comes about two hundred years too late to be meaningful. The verbalisms lag behind the facts. Nevertheless, you shall have a lawyer—or a lollipop, whichever you prefer, after I am through questioning you. If I were you, I'd take the lollipop. More nourishing."

"I won't talk without a lawyer," Don answered firmly.

"No? I'm sorry. Don, in setting up your interview I budgeted eleven minutes for nonsense. You have used up four already—no; five. When the eleven minutes are gone and you find yourself spitting out teeth, remember that I bore you no malice. Now about this matter of whether or not you will talk; there are several ways of making a man talk and each method has its fans who swear by it. Drugs, for example—nitrous oxide, scopolamine, sodium pentothal, not to mention some of the new, more subtle, and relatively non-toxic developments. Even alcohols have been used with great success by intelligence operatives. I don't like drugs; they affect the intellect and clutter up an interview with data of no use to me. You'd be amazed at the amount of rubbish that can collect in the human brain, Don, if you had had to listen to it—as I have.

"And there is hypnosis and its many variations. There is also the artificial stimulation of an unbearable need, as with morphine addiction. Finally there is old-fashioned force—pain. Why, I know an artist—I believe he is in the building now—who can successfully question the most recalcitrant case, in minimum time and using only his bare hands. Then, of course, under that category, is the extremely ancient switch in which the force, or pain, is not applied to the person being examined but to a second person whom he cannot bear to see hurt, such as a wife, or son, or daughter. Offhand, that method would seem difficult to use on you, as your only close relatives are not on this planet." The security officer glanced at his watch and added, "Only thirty seconds of nonsense still available, Don. Shall we start?"

"Huh? Wait a minute! You used up the time; I've hardly said a word."

"I haven't time to be fair. Sorry. However," he went on, "the apparent objection to the last method does not apply in your case. During the short time you were unconscious at Dr. Jefferson's apartment we were able to determine that there actually was available a—person who meets the requirements. You will talk freely rather than let this person be hurt."

"Huh?"

"A stock pony named 'Lazy.' "

The suggestion caught him completely off guard; he was stunned by it. The man went quickly on, "If you insist, we will adjourn for three hours or so and I will have your horse shipped here. It might be interesting, as I don't believe the method has ever been used with a horse before. I understand that their ears are rather sensitive. On the other hand I feel bound to tell you that, if we go to the trouble of bringing him here, we won't send him back but will simply send him to the stockyards to be butchered. Horses are an anachronism in New Chicago, don't you think?"

Don's head was whirling too much to make a proper answer, or even to follow all of the horrid implications of the comments. Finally he burst out, "You can't! You wouldn't!"

"Time's up, Don."

Don took a deep breath, collapsed. "Go ahead," he said dully. "Ask your questions."

The lieutenant took a film spool from his desk, fed it into a projector which faced back toward him. "Your name, please."

"Donald James Harvey."

"And your Venerian name?"

Don whistled "Mist on the Waters."

"Where were you born?"

"In the *Outward Bound*, in trajectory between Luna and Ganymede." The questions went on and on. Don's inquisitor appeared to have all the answers already displayed in front of him; once or twice he had Don elaborate or corrected him on some minor point. After reviewing his entire past life he required Don to give a detailed account of the events starting with his receiving the message from his parents to take passage on the *Valkyrie* for Mars.

The only thing Don left out was Dr. Jefferson's remarks about the package. He waited nervously, expecting to be hauled up short about it. But if the security policeman knew of the package, he gave no sign of it. "Dr. Jefferson seemed to think that this so-called security operative was following you? Or him?"

"I don't know. I don't think he knew."

" 'The wicked flee when no man pursueth,' " the lieutenant quoted. "Tell me exactly what you did after you left *The Back Room*."

"Was that man following me?" Don asked. "So help me,

I had never laid eyes on that dragon before; I was just passing the time of day, being polite."

"I'm sure you were. But I'll ask the questions. Go ahead."

"Well, we changed cabs twice—or maybe three times. I don't know just where we went; I don't know the city and was all turned around. But eventually we came back to Dr. Jefferson's apartment." He omitted mention of the call to the *Caravansary;* again, if his questioner was aware of the omission, he gave no sign of it.

The lieutenant said, "Well, that seems to bring us up to date." He switched off the projector and sat staring at nothing for some minutes. "Son, there is no doubt in my mind but what you are potentially disloyal."

"Why do you say that?"

"Never mind the guff. There's nothing in your background to make you loyal. But that is nothing to get excited about; a person in my position has to be practical. You are planning to leave for Mars tomorrow morning."

"I sure am!"

"Good. I don't see how you could have been up to much mischief at your age, isolated as you were out on that ranch. But you fell into bad company. Don't miss that ship; if you are still here tomorrow I might have to revise my opinions."

The lieutenant stood up and so did Don. "I'll certainly catch it!" Don agreed, then stopped. "Unless——"

"Unless what?" the lieutenant said sharply.

"Well, they held up my ticket for security clearance," Don blurted out.

"They did, eh? A routine matter; I'll take care of it. You can leave now. Open sky!"

Don did not make the conventional answer. The man said, "Don't be sulky. It would have been simpler to have beaten the living daylights out of you, then questioned you. But I didn't; I have a son about your age myself. And I never intended to hurt your horse—happens I like horses; I'm a country boy originally. No hard feelings?"

"Uh, I guess not."

The lieutenant put out his hand; Don found himself accepting it—he even found himself liking the man. He decided to chance one more question. "Could I say goodbye to Dr. Jefferson?"

The man's expression changed. "I'm afraid not."

"Why not? You'd be watching me, wouldn't you?"

The officer hesitated. "There's no reason why you shouldn't know. Dr. Jefferson was a man in very poor health. He got excited, suffered an attack and died of heart failure, earlier tonight."

Don simply stared. "Brace up!" the man said sharply. "It happens to all of us." He pressed a button on his desk; a guard came in and was told to take Don out. He was led out by another route but he was too bemused to notice it. Dr. Jefferson dead? It did not seem possible. A man so alive, so obviously in love with life— He was dumped out into a major public tunnel while still thinking about it.

Suddenly he recalled a phrase he had heard in class from his biology teacher, " 'In the end, all forms of death can be classed as heart failure.' " Don held up his right hand, stared at it. He would wash it as quickly as he could.

IV

The *Glory Road*

HE STILL had things to do; he could not stand there all night. First, he supposed that he had better go back to the station and pick up his bags. He fumbled in his pouch for his claim check while he worried about just how he would get there; he still did not have hard money with which to pay off an autocab.

He failed to find the claim check. Presently he removed everything from the pouch. Everything else was there; his letter of credit; his identification card, the messages from his parents, a flat photo of Lazy, his birth certificate, odds and ends—but no claim check. He remembered putting it there.

He thought of going back into the I.B.I warren; he was

quite sure now that it must have been taken from him while he slept. Darn funny, him falling asleep like that, at such a time. Had they drugged him? He decided against going back. Not only did he not know the name of the officer who had questioned him, nor any other way of identifying him, but more importantly he would not have gone back into that place for all the baggage in Gary Station. Let it go, let it go—he'd pick up more socks and shorts before blast off!

He decided instead to go to the *Caravansary*. First he had to find out where it was; he walked slowly along, looking for someone who did not seem too busy nor too important to ask. He found him in the person of a lottery ticket vendor at the next intersection.

The vendor looked him over. "You don't want to go to that place, Mac. I can fix you up with something really good." He winked.

Don insisted that he knew what he wanted. The man shrugged. "Okay, chump. Straight ahead until you come to a square with an electric fountain in it, then take the slidewalk south. Ask anybody where to get off. What month were you born?"

"July."

"July! Boy, are you lucky—I've just got one ticket left with your horoscope combination. Here." Don had no intention at all of buying it and he thought of telling the grifter that he considered horoscopes as silly as spectacles on a cow—but he found that he had purchased it with his last coin. He pocketed the ticket, feeling foolish. The vendor said, "About half a mile on the slidewalk. Brush the hay out of your hair before you go in."

Don found the slidewalk without difficulty and discovered that it was a pay-as-you-enter express. The machine not being interested in lottery tickets he walked the catwalk alongside it to the hotel. He had no trouble finding it; its brilliantly lighted entrance spread for a hundred yards along the tunnel.

No one scurried to help him as he came in. He went to the reservation desk and asked for a room. The clerk looked him over doubtfully. "Did someone take care of your baggage, sir?"

Don explained that he had none. "Well . . . that will be twenty-two fifty, in advance. Sign here, please."

Don signed and stamped his thumb print, then got out his father's letter of credit. "Can I get this cashed?"

"How much is it?" The clerk took it, then said, "Certainly, sir. Let me have your ID, please." Don passed it over. The clerk took it and the fresh thumb print, placed both in a comparison machine. The machine beeped agreement; the clerk handed back the card. "You are you, all right." He counted out the money, deducting the room charge. "Will your baggage be along, sir?" His manner indicated that Don's social status had jumped.

"Uh, no, but there might be some mail for me." Don explained that he was going out on the *Glory Road* in the morning.

"I'll query the mail room."

The answer was no; Don looked disappointed. The clerk said, "I'll have the mail room flag your name. If anything arrives before up-ship, you'll be sure to get it—even if we have to send a messenger to the field."

"Thanks a lot."

"Not at all. Front!" As he let himself be led away Don suddenly realized that he was groggy. The big foyer clock told him that it was already tomorrow, had been for hours—in fact he was paying seven-fifty an hour, about, for the privilege of a bed, but the way he felt he would have paid more than that simply to crawl into a hole.

He did not go immediately to bed. The *Caravansary* was a luxury hotel; even its "cheap" rooms had the minimums of civilized living. He adjusted the bath for a cycling hot sitz, threw off his clothes, and let the foaming water soothe him. After a bit he changed the pattern and floated in tepid stillness.

He came to with a start and got out. Ten minutes later, dried, powdered, and tingling with massage, he stepped back into the bedroom feeling almost restored. The ranch school had been intentionally monastic, oldstyle beds and mere showers; that bath was worth the price of the room.

The delivery chute's annunciator shone green; he opened it and found three items. The first was a largish package sealed in plastic and marked "CARAVANSARY COURTESY KIT"; it contained a comb and toothbrush, a sleeping pill, a headache powder, a story film for the bed's ceiling projector, a New Chicago *News,* and a breakfast menu. The second item was a card from his roommate; the third item was a small package, a common mailing tube. The card read: *Dear Don, A package came for you on the* P.M.—*I got the Head to let me run it into Alb-Q-Q. Squinty is taking over Lazy. Must sign off; I've got to land this heap. All the best—Jack.*

Good old Jack, he said to himself, and picked up the mailing tube. He looked at the return address and realized with something of a shock that this must be the package over which Dr. Jefferson had been so much concerned, the package which apparently had led to his death. He stared at it and wondered if it could be true that a citizen could be dragged out of his own home, then so maltreated that he died.

Was the man he had had dinner with only hours ago really dead? Or had the security cop lied to him for some reason of his own?

Part of it was certainly true; he had seen them waiting to arrest the doctor—why, he himself had been arrested and threatened and questioned, and had had his baggage virtually stolen from him, for nothing! He hadn't been doing a thing, not a confounded thing, just going about his lawful business.

Suddenly he was shaking with anger. He had let himself be pushed around; he made a solemn vow never to let it happen again. He could see now that there were half a dozen places where he should have been stubborn. If he had fought right at the outset, Dr. Jefferson might be alive—if he actually were dead, he amended.

But he had let himself be bulldozed by the odds against him. He promised himself never again to pay any attention to the odds, but only to the issues.

He controlled his trembling and opened the package.

A moment later he was looking baffled. The tube contained nothing but a man's ring, a cheap plastic affair such as one might find on any souvenir counter. An old English capital "H" framed with a circle had been pressed into the face of it and the grooves filled with white enamel. It was flashy but commonplace and of no value at all to any but the childish and vulgar in taste.

Don turned it over and over, then put it aside and sorted through its wrappings. There was nothing else, not even a message, just plain white paper used to pack the ring. Don thought it over.

The ring obviously was not the cause of the excitement; it seemed to him that there were just two possibilities: first, that the security police had switched packages—if they had, there was probably nothing he could do about it—and second, if the ring were unimportant but it was the right package, then the rest of the contents of the package must be important *even though it looked like nothing but blank paper.*

The idea that he might be carrying a message in invisible ink excited him and he started thinking of ways to bring out the message. Heat? Chemical reagents? Radiation? Even as he considered it he realized regretfully that, supposing there were such a message, it was not his place to try to make it legible; he was simply to deliver it to his father.

He decided, too, that it was more likely that this was a dummy package sent along by the police. He had no way of telling what they might have forced out of Dr. Jefferson. Which reminded him that there was still one thing he could do to check up, futile as it probably would be; he stepped to the phone and asked for Dr. Jefferson's residence. True, the doctor had told him not to phone—but the circumstances had changed.

He had to wait a bit, then the screen lighted up—and he found himself staring into the face of the security police lieutenant who had grilled him. The police officer stared back. "Oh, me!" he said in a tired voice, "so you didn't believe me? Go back to bed; you have to be up in an hour or so."

Don switched off without saying anything.

So Dr. Jefferson was either dead or still in the hands of the police. Very well; he would assume that the paper came from the doctor—and he would deliver that paper in spite of all the slimily polite stormtroopers New Chicago could muster! The dodge the doctor had apparently used to fake the purpose of the paper caused him to wonder what he could do to cover up its importance. Presently he got his stylus from his pouch, smoothed out the paper, and started a letter. The paper looked enough like writing paper to make a letter on it seem reasonable—it might be writing paper in truth. He started in "Dear Mother and Dad, I got your radiogram this morning and was I excited!" He continued, simply covering space in a sprawling hand and finishing, when he was about to run out of paper, by mentioning an intention to add to the letter and have the whole thing sent off as soon as his ship was in radio range of Mars. He then folded it, tucked it into his wallet, and put the whole into his pouch.

He looked at the clock as he finished. Good heavens! He should be up in an hour; it was hardly worthwhile going to bed. But his eyes were trying to close even as he thought it; he saw that the alarm dial of the bed was graduated from "Gentle Reminder" to "Earthquake"; he picked the extreme setting and crawled in.

He was being bounced around, a blinding light was flashing in his eyes, and a siren was running up and down the scale. Don gradually became aware of himself, scrambled out of bed. Mollified, the bed ceased its uproar.

He decided against breakfast in his room for fear that he might go back to sleep, choosing instead to stumble into his clothes and seek out the hotel's coffee shop. Four cups of coffee and a solid meal later, checked out and armed with hard money for an autocab, he headed for Gary Station. At the reservation office of Interplanet Lines he asked for his ticket. A strange clerk hunted around, then said, "I don't see it. It's not with the security clearances."

This, Don thought, is the last straw. "Look around. It's bound to be there!"

"But it's— Wait a moment!" The clerk picked up a slip. "Donald James Harvey? You're to pick up your ticket in room 4012, on the mezzanine."

"Why?"

"Search me; I just work here. That's what it says."

Mystified and annoyed, Don sought out the room named. The door was plain except for a notice "Walk In"; he did . . . and found himself again facing the security lieutenant of the night before.

The officer looked up from a desk. "Get that sour look off your puss, Don," he snapped. "I haven't had much sleep either."

"What do you want of me?"

"Take off your clothes."

"Why?"

"Because we are going to search you. You didn't really think I'd let you take off without it, did you?"

Don planted his feet. "I've had just about enough pushing around," he said slowly. "If you want my clothes off, you'll have to do it."

The police officer scowled. "I could give you a couple of convincing answers to that, but I am fresh out of patience. Kelly! Arteem! Strip him."

Three minutes later Don had an incipient black eye and was nursing a damaged arm. He decided that it was not broken, after all. The lieutenant and his assistants had disappeared into a rear room with his clothing and pouch. It occurred to him that the door behind him did not seem to be locked, but he dropped the idea; making a dash for it through Gary Station in his skin did not appear to make sense.

Despite the inevitable defeat his morale was better than it had been in hours.

The lieutenant returned presently and shoved his clothes at him. "Here you are. And here's your ticket. You may want to put on clean clothes; your bags are back of the desk."

Don accepted them silently, ignored the suggestion about a change in order to save time. While he was dressing the lieutenant said suddenly, "When did you pick up that ring?"

"Forwarded to me from school."

"Let me see it."

Don took it off and flung it at him. "Keep it, you thief!"

The lieutenant caught it and said mildly, "Now, Don, it's nothing personal." He looked the ring over carefully, then said, "Catch!" Don caught it and put it back on, picked up his bags and started to leave. "Open sky," said the lieutenant.

Don ignored him.

" 'Open sky,' I said!"

Don turned again, looked him in the eye and said, "Some day I hope to meet you socially." He went on out. They had spotted the paper after all; he had noticed that it was missing when he got back his clothes and pouch.

This time he took the precaution of getting an anti-nausea shot before up-ship. After he had stood in line for that he had barely time to be weighed in before the warning signal. As he was about to get into the elevator he saw what he believed to be a familiar figure lumbering onto the cargo lift nearby—"Sir Isaac Newton." At least it looked like his passing acquaintance of the day before, though he had to admit that the difference in appearance between one dragon and another was sometimes a bit subtle for the human eye.

He refrained from whistling a greeting; the events of the past few hours had rendered him less naive and more cautious. He thought about those events as the elevator mounted up the ship's side. It was unbelievably only twenty-four hours, less in fact, since he had gotten that radio message. It seemed like a month and he himself felt aged ten years.

Bitterly he reflected that they had outwitted him after all. Whatever message lay concealed in that wrapping paper was now gone for good. Or bad.

Couch 64 in the *Glory Road* was one of a scant half dozen on the third deck; the compartment was almost empty and there were marks on the deck where other couches had been unbolted. Don found his place and strapped his bags to the rack at its foot. While he was doing so he heard a rich Cockney voice behind him; he turned and whistled a greeting.

"Sir Isaac Newton" was being cautiously introduced into the compartment from the cargo hold below with the help of about six spaceport hands. He whistled back a courteous answer while continuing to supervise the engineering feat via voder. "Easy, friends, easy does it! Now if two of you will be so kind as to place my left midships foot on the ladder, bearing in mind that I cannot see it— Wups! mind your fingers. There, I think I can make it now. Is there anything breakable in the way of my tail?"

The boss stevedore answered, "All clear, chief. Upsy-daisy!"

"If you mean what I think you mean," answered the Venerian, "then, 'On your mark; get set—GO!' " There was a crunching metallic sound, a tinkle of breaking glass, and the huge saurian scrambled up out of the hatch. Once there he turned cautiously around and settled himself in the space left vacant for him. The spaceport hands followed him and secured him to the deck with steel straps. He waggled an eye at the straw boss. "You, I take it, are the chieftain of this band?"

"I'm in charge."

The Venerian's tendrils quitted the keys of the voder, sought out a pouch by it, and removed a sheaf of paper money. He laid it on the deck and returned to the keys. "Then, sir, will you favor me by accepting this evidence of my gratitude for a difficult service well performed and distribute it among your assistants equitably and according to your customs, whatever they may be?"

The human scooped it up and shoved it into his pouch. "Sure thing, chief. Thanks."

"The honor is mine." The laborers left and the dragon turned his attention to Don, but, before they could exchange any words, the last of the compartment's human freight came down from the deck above. It was a family party; the female head thereof took one look inside and screamed.

She swarmed back up the ladder, causing a traffic jam with her descendants and spouse as she did so. The dragon swiveled two eyes in her direction while waving the others at Don. "Dear me!" he keyed. "Do you think it would help if I were to assure the lady that I have no anthropophagic tendencies?"

Don felt acutely embarrassed; he wished for some way to disown the woman as a blood sister and member of his race. "She's just a stupid fool," he answered. "Please don't pay any attention to her."

"I fear me that a merely negative approach will not suffice."

Don whistled an untranslatable dragon sound of contempt and continued with *"May her life be long and tedious."*

"Tut, tut," the dragon tapped back. "Unreasoned anguish is nonetheless real. 'To understand all is to forgive all'—one of your philosophers."

Don did not recognize the quotation and it seemed pretty extreme to him, in any case. He was sure that there were things he would never forgive no matter how well he understood them—some recent events, in fact. He was about to say so when both their attentions were arrested by sounds pouring down the open hatchway. Two and perhaps more male voices were engaged in an argument with a shrill female voice rising over them and sometimes drowning them out. It appeared (a) that she wanted to speak to the captain (b) that she had been carefully brought up and had never had to put up with such things (c) that those hideous monsters should never be allowed to come to Earth; they should be exterminated (d) that if Adolf were half a man he wouldn't just stand there and let his own wife be treated so (e) she intended to write to the company and that her family was not without influence and (f) that she *demanded* to speak to the captain.

Don wanted to say something to cover it up but he was fascinated by it. Presently the sounds moved away and died out; a ship's officer came down the hatch and looked around. "Are you comfortable?" he said to "Sir Isaac Newton."

"Quite, thank you."

He turned to Don. "Get your bags, young man, and come with me. The captain has decided to give his nibs here a compartment to himself."

"Why?" asked Don. "My ticket says couch sixty-four and I like it here."

The ship's officer scratched his chin and looked at him, then turned to the Venerian. "Is it all right with you?"

"Most certainly. I shall be honored by the young gentleman's company."

He turned back to Don. "Well . . . all right. I'd probably

have to hang you on a hook if I moved you anyway." He glanced at his watch and swore. "If I don't get a move on, we'll miss take-off and have to lay over a day." He was up and out of the compartment as he spoke.

The final warning sounded over the announcing system; a hoarse voice followed it with, "All hands! Strap down! Stand by for lift—" The order was followed by a transcription of the brassy strains of Le Compte's *Raise Ship!* Don's pulse quickened; excitement mounted in him. He felt ecstatically happy, eager to be back in space again, back where he belonged. The bad, confusing things of the past day washed out of his mind; even the ranch and Lazy grew dim.

So timed was the transcribed music that the rocket-blast effect of the final chorus merged into the real blast of the ship's tubes; the *Glory Road* stirred and lifted . . . then threw herself away into the open sky.

V

Circum-Terra

THE WEIGHT of acceleration was no worse than it had been the day before in the *Santa Fé Trail* but the drive persisted for more than five minutes, minutes that seemed like an endless hour. After they passed the speed of sound the compartment was relatively quiet. Don made a great effort and managed to turn his head a little. "Sir Isaac Newton's" great bulk was flattened to the deck, making Don think unpleasantly of a lizard crushed into a road. His eyestalks drooped like limp asparagus. He looked dead.

Don strained for breath and called out, "Are you all right?"

The Venerian did not stir. His voder instrument was covered by the sagging folds of his neck; it seemed unlikely that his tendrils could have managed the delicate touch required for its keys even had it been free. Nor did he reply in his own whistling speech.

Don wanted to go to him, but he was as immobilized by the blast weight as is the bottommost player in a football pile up. He forced his head back where it belonged so that he might breathe less painfully and waited.

When the blast died away his stomach gave one protesting flipflop, then quieted down; either the anti-nausea shot had worked or he had his space balance again—or both. Without waiting for permission from the control room he quickly unstrapped and hurried to the Venerian. He steadied himself in the air, holding with one hand to the steel bands restraining his companion.

The dragon was no longer crushed to the deckplates; only the steel hoops kept him from floating around the compartment. Behind him his giant tail waved loosely, brushing the ship's plates and knocking off paint chips.

The eyestalks were still limp and each eye filmed over. The dragon stirred only in the meaningless motion of string in water; there was nothing to show that he was alive. Don clenched a fist and pounded on the creature's flat skull. "Can you hear me? Are you all right?"

All he got out of it was a bruised hand; Sir Isaac made no response. Don hung for a moment, wondering what to do. That his acquaintance was in a bad way he felt sure, but his training in first aid did not extend to Venerian pseudo-saurians. He dug back into his childhood memories, trying to think of something.

The same ship's officer who had rearranged the berthing appeared at the forward or "upper" hatch, floating head "down." "All okay this deck?" he inquired perfunctorily and started to back out.

"No!" Don shouted. "Case of blast shock."

"Huh?" The officer swam on into the compartment and looked at the other passenger. He swore unimaginatively and looked worried. "This is beyond me; I never carried one before. How the deuce do you give artificial respiration to a thing as big as that?"

"You don't," Don told him. "His lungs are completely enclosed in his armor box."

"He looks dead. I think he's stopped breathing."

A memory floated to the top in Don's mind; he snatched it. "Got a cigarette?"

"Huh? Don't bother me! Anyhow the smoking lamp is out."

"You don't understand," Don persisted. "If you've got one, light it. You can blow smoke at his nostril plate and see whether or not he's breathing."

"Oh. Well, maybe it's a good idea." The spaceman got out a cigarette and struck it.

"But be careful," Don went on. "They can't stand nicotine. One big puff and then put it out."

"Maybe it's not such a good idea," the ship's officer objected. "Say, you sound like a Venus colonial?"

Don hesitated, then answered, "I'm a Federation citizen." It seemed like a poor time to discuss politics. He moved over to the dragon's chin, braced his feet against the deckplates and shoved, thus exposing the Venerian's nostril plate which was located under the creature's head in the folds of his neck. Don could not have managed it, save that they were in free fall, making the bulky mass weightless.

The man blew smoke at the exposed opening. It eddied forward, then some of it curled inside; the dragon was still alive.

Still very much alive. Every eyestalk sprang to rigid attention; he lifted his chin, carrying Don with it, then he sneezed. The blast struck Don where he floated loosely and turned him over and over. He threshed in the air for a moment before catching a handhold on the hatch ladder.

The ship's officer was rubbing one wrist. "The beggar clipped me," he complained. "I won't try that again soon. Well, I guess he'll be all right."

Sir Isaac whistled mournfully; Don answered him. The spaceman looked at him. "You savvy that stuff?"

"Some."

"Well, tell him to use his squawk box. I don't!"

Don said, "Sir Isaac—use your voder."

The Venerian tried to comply. His tentacles hunted around, found the keys of the artificial voice box, and touched them.

No sounds came out. The dragon turned an eye at Don and whistled a series of phrases.

"He regrets to say that its spirit has departed," Don interpreted.

The ship's officer sighed. "I wonder why I ever left the grocery business? Well, if we can get it unlatched from him, I'll see if 'Sparks' can fix it."

"Let me," said Don and squirmed into the space between the dragon's head and the deckplates. The voder case, he found, was secured to four rings riveted to the Venerian's skin plates. He could not seem to find the combination; the dragon's tendrils fluttered over his hands, moved them gently out of the way, unfastened the box, and handed it to him. He wiggled out and gave it to the man. "Looks like he kind of slept on it," he commented.

"A mess," the other agreed. "Well, tell him I'll have them fix it if possible and that I'm glad he wasn't hurt."

"Tell him yourself; he understands English."

"Eh? Oh, of course, of course." He faced the Venerian who immediately set up a long shrilling. "What's he say?"

Don listened. "He says he appreciates your good wishes but that he is sorry to have to disagree; he is unwell. He says that he urgently requires—" Don stopped and looked puzzled, then whistled the Venerian equivalent of "Say that again, please?"

Sir Isaac answered him; Don went on, "He says he's just got to have some sugar syrup."

"Huh?"

"That's what he says."

"I'll be— How much?"

There was another exchange of whistles; Don answered, "Uh, he says he needs at least a quarter of a—there isn't any word for it; it's an amount about equal to half a barrel, I'd say."

"You mean he wants *half a barrel* of waffle juice?"

"No, no, a quarter of that—an eighth of a barrel. What would that come to in gallons?"

"I wouldn't attempt it without a slipstick; I'm confused. I don't even know that we have any on board." Sir Isaac set up more frantic whistling. "But if we don't, I'll have the cook whop up some. Tell him to hold everything and take it easy." He scowled at the dragon, then left quite suddenly.

Don attached himself to one of the steel straps and asked, "How are you feeling now?"

The dragon replied apologetically to the effect that he needed to return to the egg for the moment. Don shut up and waited.

The captain himself showed up to attend the sick passenger. The ship, being in free trajectory for the satellite space station, would not require his presence in the control room until well past noon, New Chicago time; he was free to move around the ship. He arrived in company with the ship's doctor and followed by a man herding a metal tank.

The two conferred over the dragon, at first ignoring Don's presence. However neither of them knew the piping speech of the dragon tribe; they were forced to turn to Don. Through him Sir Isaac again insisted that he required sugar solution as a stimulant. The captain looked worried. "I've read somewhere that sugar gets them drunk the same as alcohol does us."

Don again translated for the Venerian; what he had asked for was simply a medicinal dose.

The captain turned to the medical officer. "How about it, surgeon?"

The doctor stared at the bulkhead. "Captain, this is as far outside my duties as tap dancing."

"Confound it, man, I asked for your official opinion!"

The medical officer faced him. "Very well, sir—I would say that if this passenger should die, you having refused him something he had asked for, it would look very, very bad indeed."

The captain bit his lip. "As you say, sir. But I'll be switched if I want several tons of intoxicated dragon banging around in my ship. Administer the dose."

"Me, sir?"

"*You*, sir."

The ship being in free fall it was quite impossible to pour out the syrup and let the Venerian lick it up, nor was he physically equipped to use the "baby bottle" drinking bladders used by humans when weightless. But that had been anticipated; the tank containing the syrup was a type used in the galley to handle soup or coffee in free fall. It had a hand pump and an attachable hose.

It was decided, Sir Isaac concurring, to place the end of the hose well down the dragon's throat. But nobody seemed to want the job. Granted that *Draco Veneris Wilsonii* is a civilized race, to stick one's head and shoulders between those rows of teeth seemed to be inviting a breach in foreign relations.

Don volunteered for the job and was sorry when they took him up on it. He trusted Sir Isaac but recalled times when Lazy had stepped on his foot quite unintentionally. He hoped that the dragon had no unfortunate involuntary reflexes; apologies are no use to a corpse.

While he kept the end of the hose firmly in place he held his breath and was glad that he had taken that antinausea injection. Sir Isaac did not have halitosis, as dragons go, but dragons go rather far in that direction. The job done, he was happy to back out.

Sir Isaac thanked them all, via Don, and assured them that he would now recover rapidly. He seemed to fall asleep in the midst of whistling. The ship's doctor peeled one eyestalk and shined a hand torch at it. "The stuff has hit him, I think. We'll let him be and hope for the best."

They all left. Don looked his friend over, decided that there was no point in sitting up with him, and followed them. The compartment had no view port; he wanted at least one good look at Earth while they were still close by. He found what he sought three decks forward.

They were still only fifteen thousand miles out; Don had to crowd in close to the view port to see all of Earth at one time. It was, he had to admit, a mighty pretty planet; he was a little bit sorry to be leaving it. Hanging there against velvet black and pinpoint stars, drenched in sunlight so bright it hurt your eyes, it almost took your breath away.

The sunrise line had swung far into the Pacific past Hawaii, and North America was spread out to his gaze. Storm blanketed the Pacific Northwest, but the Midwest was fairly clear and the Southwest was sharp. He could make out where New Chicago was with ease; he could see the Grand Canyon and from it he could almost figure out where the ranch had to be. He was sure that with a small telescope he could have spotted it.

He gave up his place at last. He was soaking in the pleasant melancholy of mild homesickness and the comments of some of the other passengers were beginning to annoy him—not the cheerful inanities of tourists but the know-it-all remarks of self-appointed old timers, making their second trip out. He headed back to his own compartment.

He was startled to hear his name called. He turned and the ship's officer he had met before floated up to him. He had with him Sir Isaac's voder. "You seem to be chummy with that over-educated crocodile you're bunking with; how about taking this to him?"

"Why, certainly."

"The radio officer says it needs an overhaul but at least it's working again." Don accepted it and went aft. The dragon seemed to be sleeping, then one eye waved at him and Sir Isaac whistled a salutation.

"I've got your voice box," Don told him. "Want me to fasten it on for you?"

Sir Isaac politely refused. Don handed the instrument to the fidgeting tendrils and the dragon arranged it to suit him. He then ran over the keys as a check, producing sounds like frightened ducks. Satisfied, he began to speak in English: "I am enriched by the debt you have placed upon me."

"It was nothing," Don answered. "I ran into the mate a couple of decks forward and he asked me to fetch it along."

"I do not refer to this artificial voice, but to your ready help when I was in distress and peril. Without your quick wit, your willingness to share mud with an untested stranger, and—in passing—your knowledge of the true speech, I might have lost my chance to attain the happy death."

"Shucks," Don answered, feeling somewhat pink, "it was a pleasure." He noticed that the dragon's speech was slow and somewhat slurred, as if his tentacles lacked their customary dexterity. Besides that, Sir Isaac's talk was more pedantic than ever and much more Cockney-flavored—the voder was mixing aspirates with abandon and turning the *theta* sound into "f"; Don felt sure that the Earthman who had taught him to speak must have been born in earshot of Bow Bells.

He noticed as well that his friend could not seem to make up his mind which eye he wanted to use on him. He kept waggling one after another at Don, as if seeking one which would let him focus better. Don wondered if Sir Isaac had overestimated the proper size of a medicinal dose.

"Permit me," the Venerian went on, still with ponderous dignity, "to judge the worth of the service you have done me." He changed the subject. "This word 'shucks'—I do not recognize the use you made of it. Husks of plants?"

Don struggled to explain how little and how much "shucks" could mean. The dragon thought it over and tapped out an answer. "I believe that I gain a portion of understanding. The semantic content of this word is emotional and variable, rather than orderly and descriptive. Its referent is the state of one's spirits?"

"That's it," Don said happily. "It means just what you want it to mean. It's the way you say it."

"Shucks," the dragon said experimentally. "Shucks. I seem to be getting the feel of it. A delightful word. Shucks." He went on, "The delicate nuances of speech must be learned from the living users thereof. Perhaps I may return the favor by helping you in some small wise with your already great mastery of the speech of my people? Shucks."

This confirmed Don's suspicion that his own whistling had become so villainous that it might do for popcorn vending but not for regular communication. "I certainly would appreciate a chance to brush up," he answered. "I haven't had a chance to speak 'true speech' for years—not since I was a kid. I was taught by a historian who was working with my father on the (whistled) ruins. Perhaps you know him? His name was 'Professor Charles Darwin.'" Don added the whistled or true version of the Venerian scholar's name.

"You ask me if I know (whistled)? He is my brother; his grandmother, nine times removed, and my grandmother, seven times removed, were the same egg. Shucks!" He added, "A learned person, for one so young."

Don was a bit taken aback to hear "Professor Darwin" described as "young"; as a child he had classed him and the ruins as being about the same age. He now had to remind himself that Sir Isaac might see it differently. "Say, that's nice!" he answered. "I wonder if you knew my parents? Dr. Jonas Harvey and Dr. Cynthia Harvey?"

The dragon turned all eyes on him. "You are their egg? I have not had the honor of meeting them but all civilized persons know of them and their work. I am no longer surprised at your own excellence. Shucks!"

Don felt both embarrassment and pleasure. Not knowing what to say he suggested that Sir Isaac coach him for a while in "true speech," a suggestion to which the dragon readily assented. They were still so engaged when the warning signal sounded and a voice from the control room sang out, "Strap down for acceleration! Prepare to match trajectories!"

Don placed his hands against his friend's armored sides and shoved himself back to his coach. He paused there and said, "Are you going to be all right?"

The dragon made a sound which Don construed as a hiccup, and tapped out, "I feel sure of it. This time I am fortified."

"I hope so. Say—you don't want to bung up your voder again. Want me to take care of it?"

"If you will, please."

Don went back and got it, then fastened it to his bags. He had barely time to fasten his safety belts when the first surge of acceleration hit them. It was not so bad, this time, neither as many gravities as the blast-off from Earth nor of as long duration, for they were not breaking free of Earth's crushing grip but merely adjusting trajectories—modifying the outer end of the *Glory Road*'s elliptical path to make it agree perfectly with the circular orbit of Circum-Terra, the cross-roads station in space which was their destination.

The captain gave them one long powerful shove, waited, then blasted twice more for short intervals—without, Don noted, finding it necessary to invert and blast back. He nodded approval. Good piloting!—the captain knew his vectors. The bull horn sang out, "Contact! Unstrap at will. Prepare to disembark."

Don returned the voder to Sir Isaac, then lost track of him, for the dragon again had to be taken aft to be transferred through the cargo hatch. Don whistled goodbye and went forward, towing his bags behind him, to go out through the passenger tube.

Circum-Terra was a great confused mass in the sky. It had been built, rebuilt, added to, and modified over the course of years for a dozen different purposes—weather observation station, astronomical observatory, meteor count station, television relay, guided missile control station, high-vacuum strain-free physics laboratory, strain-free germ-free biological experiment station, and many other uses.

But most importantly it was a freight and passenger transfer station in space, the place where short-range winged rockets from Earth met the space liners that plied between the planets. For this purpose it had fueling tanks, machine shops, repair cages that could receive the largest liners and the smallest rockets, and a spinning, pressurized drum—"Goddard Hotel"—which provided artificial gravity and Earth atmosphere for passengers and for the permanent staff of Circum-Terra.

Goddard Hotel stuck out from the side of Circum-Terra like a cartwheel from a pile of junk. The hub on which it turned ran through its center and protruded out into space. It was to this hub that a ship would couple its passenger tube when discharging or loading humans. That done, the ship would then be warped over to a cargo port in the non-spinning major body of the station. When the *Glory Road* made contact, there were three other ships in at Circum-Terra, the *Valkyrie* in which Don Harvey had passage for Mars, the *Nautilus*, just in from Venus and in which Sir Isaac expected to return home, and the *Spring Tide*, the Luna shuttle which alternated with its sister the *Neap Tide*.

The two liners and the moon ship were already tied up to the main body of the station; the *Glory Road* warped in at the hub of the hotel and immediately began to discharge passengers. Don waited his turn and then pulled himself along by handholds, dragging his bags behind him, and soon found himself inside the hotel, but still in weightless free fall in the cylindrical hub of the Goddard.

A man in coveralls directed Don and the dozen passengers he was with to a point halfway along the hub where a large lift blocked further progress. Its circular door stood open and turned very slowly around, moving with the spinning hotel proper. "Get in," he ordered. "Mind you get your feet pointed toward the floor."

Don got in with the others and found that the inside of the car was cubical. One wall was marked in big letters: FLOOR. Don found a handhold and steadied himself so that his feet would be on the floor when weight was applied. The man got in and started the car out toward the rim.

There was no feeling of weight at first, at least not toward the "floor." Don experienced a dizzy sensation as increasing spin sloshed the liquid about in his inner ear. He knew that he had ridden this elevator before, when he was eleven and heading for Earth and school, but he had forgotten its unpleasant aspects.

Soon the elevator stopped; the floor became the floor in earnest, though with considerably less than one gravity, and the upsetting sensation ceased. The operator opened the door and shouted, "Everybody out!"

Don walked into a large inner compartment, carrying his bags. It was already crowded with more than half of the ship's passengers. Don looked around for his dragon friend, then remembered that the ship would have to be moved around to a cargo port before the Venerian could disembark. He put his bags on the floor and sat down on them.

The crowd, for some reason, seemed unquiet. Don heard one woman say, "This is preposterous! We've been here at least half an hour and no one appears to know that we're here."

A man answered, "Be patient, Martha."

" 'Patient' he says! Only one door out of the place and it locked—suppose there were a fire?"

"Well, where would you run to, dear? Nothing outside but some mighty thin vacuum."

She squealed. "Oh! We should have gone to Bermuda as I wanted to."

"As *you* wanted to?"

"Don't be petty!"

Another elevator load discharged and then another; the ship was empty. After many minutes more of grumbling, during which even Don began to wonder at the service, the only door other than the elevator door opened. Instead of a hotelman anxious to please his guests, in came three men in uniform. The two flank men were carrying mob guns cradled at their hips; the third man had only a hand pistol, still holstered. He stepped forward, planted his feet and set his fists on his hips. "Attention! Quiet, everybody."

He got it; his voice had the ring of command which is obeyed without thinking. He went on, "I am Assault Sergeant McMasters of the High Guard, Venus Republic. My commanding officer has directed me to advise you of the present situation."

There was an additional short moment of silence, then a rising mutter of surprise, alarm, disbelief, and indignation. "Pipe down!" the sergeant shouted. "Take it easy. Nobody's going to get hurt—if you behave." He went on, "The Republic has taken over this station and everybody is being cleared out. You groundhogs will be shipped back to Earth at once. Those of you who are headed home to Venus will go home—provided you pass our loyalty check. Now, let's get sorted out."

A fussy, plump man pushed his way forward. "Do you realize, sir, what you are saying? 'Venus Republic,' indeed. This is piracy!"

"Get back in line, fatty."

"You can't do this. I wish to speak to your commanding officer."

"Fatty," the sergeant said slowly, "back up before you get a boot in your belly." The man looked dumbfounded, then scuttled back into the crowd.

The sergeant continued, "Those of you going to Venus

form a queue here at the door. Have your ID's and birth certificates ready."

The passengers, up to that time a friendly group of fellow travelers, split into hostile camps. Someone shouted, "Long live the Republic!", which was followed by the beefy sound of a fist striking flesh. One of the guards hurried into the crowd and stopped the impending riot. The sergeant drew his sidearm and said in a bored voice, "No politics, please. Let's get on with the job."

Somehow a line was formed. The second in line was the man who had cheered the new nation. His nose was dripping blood but his eyes were shining. As he offered his papers to the sergeant he said, "This is a great day! I've waited all my life for it."

"Who hasn't?" the sergeant answered. "Okay—on through the door for processing. Next!"

Don was busy trying to quiet down and arrange his whirling thoughts. He was forced at last to admit that this was it, this was war, the war that he had told himself was impossible. No cities had been bombed, not yet—but this was the Fort Sumter of a new war; he was smart enough to see that. He did not have to be threatened with a boot in the belly to see what was in front of his face.

He realized with nervous shock that he had just barely gotten away in time. The *Valkyrie* might be the last ship to Mars in a long, long time. With the transfer station in the hands of the rebels it might be the last one for years.

The sergeant had not said anything about passengers for Mars as yet; Don told himself that the sergeant's first effort must naturally be to sort out the citizens of the two belligerents. He decided that the thing to do was to keep his mouth shut and wait.

There was an interruption in the queue. Don heard the sergeant say, "You're in the wrong pew, bud. You go back to Earth."

The man he was speaking to answered, "No, no! Take a look at my papers; I'm emigrating to Venus."

"You're a leetle bit late to be emigrating. The situation has changed."

"Why? Sure, I know it has changed. I declare for Venus."

The sergeant scratched his head. "This one isn't in the book. Atkinson! Pass this man on through; we'll let the lieutenant figure it out."

When he had completed the group that wanted to go to Venus the sergeant went to a speech-only wall phone. "Jim? Mac speaking, from the nursery. They got that dragon out yet? No? Well, let me know when the *Road* is back at the chute; I want to load." He turned back to the crowd. "All right, you groundhogs—there'll be a delay so I'm going to move you into another room until we're ready to send you back to Earth."

"Just a moment, Sergeant!" called out a male passenger.

"Yeah? What do you want?"

"Where do passengers for Luna wait?"

"Huh? Service discontinued. You're going back to Earth."

"Now, Sergeant, let's be reasonable. I haven't the slightest interest in politics; it does not matter to me who administers this station. But I have business on the Moon. It is *essential* that I get to the Moon. A delay would cost millions!"

The sergeant stared at him. "Now isn't that just too bad! You know, brother, I've never had as much as a thousand at one time in my life; the thought of losing millions scares me." His manner suddenly changed. "You stupid jerk, have you ever thought what a bomb would do to the roof of Tycho City? Now line up, all of you, double file."

Don listened to this with disquiet. Still, the sergeant had not said anything about Mars. He got into line, but at the very end. When the tail of the line reached the door he stopped. "Get a move on, kid," said the sergeant.

"I'm not going back to Earth," Don told him.

"Huh?"

"I'm headed for Mars in the *Valkyrie.*"

"Oh, I see. You mean you were—now you're headed back to Earth in the *Glory Road.*"

Don said stubbornly, "Look, mister, I've *got* to get to Mars. My parents are there; they are expecting me."

The sergeant shook his head. "Kid, I feel sorry for you. I really do. The *Valkyrie* isn't going to Mars."

"What?"

"She's being recommissioned as a cruiser of the High Guard. She's going to Venus. So I guess you had better go back to Earth. I'm sorry you won't be able to join your folks, but war is like that."

Don breathed slowly and forced himself to count up to ten. "I'm not going back to Earth. I'll wait right here until a ship does go to Mars."

The sergeant sighed. "If you do, you'll have to chin yourself on a star while you wait."

"Huh? What do you mean?"

"Because," he said slowly, "a few minutes after we blast off there will be nothing in this neighborhood but a nice, pretty radioactive cloud. Want to play a leading role in a Geiger counter?"

VI

The Sign in the Sky

DON COULD not answer. His simian ancestors, beset with perils every moment of life, might have taken it calmly; Don's soft life had not prepared him for such repeated blows. The sergeant went on, "So it had better be the *Glory Road* for you, kid. That's what your parents would want. Go back and find yourself a nice spot in the country; the cities are likely to be unhealthy for a while."

Don snapped out of it. "I'm not going back to Earth! I don't belong there; I'm not a native of Earth."

"Eh? What is your citizenship? Not that it matters; anybody who isn't a citizen of Venus goes back in the *Glory Road*."

"I'm a Federation citizen," Don answered, "but I can claim Venus citizenship."

"The Federation," the sergeant answered, "has had a slump in its stock lately. But what's this about Venus citizenship? Stow the double-talk and let's see your papers."

Don passed them over. Sergeant McMasters looked first

at his birth certificate, then stared at it. "Born in free fall! I'll be a cross-eyed pilot—say, there aren't many like you, are there?"

"I guess not."

"But just what does that make you?"

"Read on down. My mother was born on Venus. I'm Venus native born, by derivation."

"But your pop was born on Earth."

"I'm native born there, too."

"Huh? That's silly."

"That's the law."

"There are going to be some new laws. I don't know just where you fit. See here—where do you want to go? Venus or Earth?"

"I'm going to Mars," Don answered simply.

The sergeant looked at him and handed back the papers. "It beats me. And I can't get any sense out of you. I'm going to refer it on up. Come along."

He led Don down a passageway and into a small compartment which had been set up as an orderly room. Two other soldiers were there; one was using a typer, the other was just sitting. The sergeant stuck his head in and spoke to the one who was loafing. "Hey, Mike—keep an eye on this character. See that he doesn't steal the station." He turned back to Don. "Give me those papers again, kid." He took them and went away.

The soldier addressed as Mike stared at Don, then paid no further attention to him. Don put his bags down and sat on them.

After several minutes Sergeant McMasters returned but ignored Don. "Who's got the cards?" he inquired.

"I have."

"Not your readers, Mike. Where are the honest cards?" The third soldier closed the typer, reached in a drawer and pulled out a deck of cards. The three sat down at the desk and McMasters started to shuffle. He turned to Don. "Care for a friendly game, kid?"

"Uh, I guess not."

"You'll never learn any cheaper." The soldiers played cards for half an hour or so while Don kept quiet and thought. He forced himself to believe that the sergeant knew what he was talking about; he could not go to Mars in the *Valkyrie* because the *Valkyrie* was not going to Mars. He could not wait for a later ship because the station—this very room he was sitting in—was about to be blown up.

What did that leave? Earth? No! He had no relatives on Earth, none close enough to turn to. With Dr. Jefferson dead or missing he had no older friends. Perhaps he could crawl back to the ranch, tail between his legs——

No! He had outgrown that skin and shed it. The ranch school was no longer for him.

Down inside was another and stronger reason: the security police in New Chicago had made of him an alien; he would not go back because Earth was no longer his.

Hobson's choice, he told himself; it's got to be Venus. I can find people there whom I used to know—or know Dad and Mother. I'll scrounge around and find some way to get from there to Mars; that's best. His mind made up, he was almost content.

The office phone called out: "Sergeant McMasters!" The sergeant laid down his hand and went to it, pulling the privacy shield into place. Presently he switched off and turned to Don. "Well, kid, the Old Man has settled your status; you're a 'displaced person.'"

"Huh?"

"The bottom fell out for you when Venus became an independent republic. You have no citizenship anywhere. So the Old Man says to ship you back where you come from . . . back to Earth."

Don stood up and squared his shoulders. "I won't go."

"You won't, eh?" McMasters said mildly. "Well, just sit back down and be comfortable. When the time comes, we'll drag you." He started to deal the cards again.

Don did not sit down. "See here, I've changed my mind. If I can't get to Mars right away, then I'll go to Venus."

McMasters stopped and turned around. "When Commodore Higgins settles a point, it's settled. Mike, take this prima donna across and shove him in with the other groundhogs."

"But——"

Mike stood up. "Come on, you."

Don found himself shoved into a room packed with injured feelings. The Earthlings had no guards and no colonials in with them; they were giving vent freely to their opinions about events. "—outrage! We should blast every one of their settlements, level them to the ground!" "—I think we should send a committee to this commanding officer of theirs and say to him firmly—" "I *told* you we shouldn't have come!" "Negotiate? That's a sign of weakness." "Don't you realize that the war is already over? Man, this place isn't just a traffic depot; it's the main guided-missile control station. They can bomb every last city on Earth from here, like ducks on a pond!"

Don noticed the last remark, played it over in his mind, let it sink in. He was not used to thinking in terms of military tactics; up to this moment the significance of a raid on Circum-Terra had been lost on him. He had thought of it in purely personal terms, his own convenience.

Would they actually go that far? Bomb the Federation cities right off the map? Sure, the colonials had plenty to be sore about, but— Of course, it had happened like that, once in the past, but that was history; people were more civilized now. Weren't they?

"Harvey! Donald Harvey!"

Everyone turned at the call. A Venus Guardsman was standing in the compartment door, shouting his name. Don answered, "Here."

"Come along."

Don picked up his bags and followed him out into the passageway, waited while the soldier relocked the door. "Where are you taking me?"

"The C. O. wants to see you." He glanced at Don's baggage. "No need to drag that stuff."

"Uh, I guess I'd better keep it with me."

"Suit yourself. But don't take it into the C. O.'s office." He took Don down two decks where the "gravity" was appreciably greater and stopped at a door guarded by a sentry. "Here's the guy the Old Man sent for—Harvey."

"Go right on in."

Don did so. The room was large and ornate; it had been

the office of the hotel manager. Now it was occupied by a man in uniform, a man still young though his hair was shot with grey. He looked up as Don came in; Don thought he looked alert but tired. "Donald Harvey?"

"Yes, sir." Don got out his papers.

The commanding officer brushed them aside. "I've seen them. Harvey, you are a headache to me. I disposed of your case once."

Don did not answer; the other went on, "Now it appears that I must reopen it. Do you know a Venerian named—" He whistled it.

"Slightly," Don answered. "We shared a compartment in the *Glory Road*."

"Hmm. . . . I wonder if you planned it that way?"

"What? How could I?"

"It could have been arranged . . . and it would not be the first time that a young person has been used as a spy."

Don turned red. "You think I am a spy, sir?"

"No, it is just one of the possibilities I must consider. No military commander enjoys political pressure being used on him, Harvey, but they all have to yield to it. I've yielded. You aren't going back to Earth; you are going to Venus." He stood up. "But let me warn you; if you are a ringer who has been planted on me, all the dragons on Venus won't save your skin." He turned to a ship's phone, punched its keys, and waited; presently he said, "Tell him his friend is here and that I've taken care of the matter." He turned back to Don. "Take it."

Shortly Don heard a warm Cockney voice, "Don, my dear boy, are you there?"

"Yes, Sir Isaac."

The dragon shrilled relief. "When I inquired about you, I found some preposterous intention of shipping you back to that dreadful place we just quitted. I told them that a mistake had been made. I'm afraid I had to be quite firm about it. Shucks!"

"It's all fixed up now, Sir Isaac. Thanks."

"Not at all; I am still in your debt. Come to visit me when it is possible. You will, won't you?"

"Oh, sure!"

"Thank you and cheerio! Shucks."

Don turned away from the phone to find the task force commander studying him quizzically. "Do you know who your friend is?"

"Who he is?" Don whistled the Venerian name, then added, "He calls himself 'Sir Isaac Newton.' "

"That's all you know?"

"I guess so."

"Mmm—" He paused, then went on, "You might as well know what influenced me. 'Sir Isaac,' as you call him, traces his ancestry directly back to the Original Egg, placed in the mud of Venus on the day of Creation. So that's why I'm stuck with you. Orderly!"

Don let himself be led away without saying a word. Few if any Earthlings have been converted to the dominant religion of Venus; it is not a proselyting faith. But none laugh at it; all take it seriously. A terrestrial on Venus may not believe in the Divine Egg and all that that implies; he finds it more profitable—and *much* safer—to speak of it with respect.

Sir Isaac a Child of the Egg! Don felt the sheepish awe that is likely to strike even the most hard-boiled democrat when he first comes in contact with established royalty. Why, he had been talking to him, just as if he were any old dragon—say one that sold vegetables in the city market.

Shortly he began to think of it in more practical ways. If anyone could wangle a way for him to get to Mars, Sir Isaac was probably just the bird who could do it. He turned it over in his mind—he'd get home yet!

But Don did not get to see his Venerian friend at once. He was herded into the *Nautilus* along with Venus-bound passengers from the *Glory Road* and a handful of technicians from Circum-Terra whose loyalties lay with Venus rather than with Earth. By the time he discovered that Sir Isaac had been transshipped to the *Valkyrie* it was too late to do anything about it.

The flag of the task force commander, High Commodore Higgins, was shifted from Circum-Terra back to the *Nautilus*, and Higgins moved at once to carry out the rest of the coup. The storming of Circum-Terra had been managed almost without bloodshed; it had depended on timing and surprise. Now the rest of the operation must be completed before any dislocation in ship schedules would be noticed on Earth.

The *Nautilus* and the *Valkyrie* had already been prepared for their long jumps; the *Spring Tide*'s crew was removed to be sent to Earth and a crew supplied from the task force; she herself was fueled and provisioned for deep space. Although designed for the short jump to Luna, she was quite capable of making the trip to Venus. Space travel is not a matter of distance but of gravity potential levels; the jump from Circum-Terra to Venus required less expenditure of energy than did the terrible business of fighting up though Earth's field from New Chicago to Circum-Terra.

The *Spring Tide* shoved off in a leisurely, economical parabola; she would make the trip to Venus in free fall all the way. The *Valkyrie* blasted away to shape a fast, almost flat, hyperboloid orbit; she would arrive as soon or sooner than the *Nautilus*. The *Nautilus* was last to leave, for High Commodore Higgins had one more thing to do before destroying the station—a television broadcast on a globe-wide network.

All global broadcasts originated in, or were relayed through, the communications center of Circum-Terra. Since the *Nautilus* had touched in at Circum-Terra, a cosmic Trojan horse, the regular broadcasts had been allowed to continue uninterrupted. The commodore's G-6 staff officer (propaganda and nerve warfare) picked as the time for the commodore's announcement to Earth of the coup the time ordinarily given over to "*Steve Brodie Says:*", the most widely heard global news commentator. Mr. Brodie immediately followed the immensely popular "Kallikak Family" serial drama, an added advantage audience-wise.

The *Glory Road* had been allowed at last to blast off for Earth with her load of refugees but with her radios wrecked. The *Nautilus* lay off in space, a hundred miles outside, hanging in a parking orbit, waiting. Inside the space station, now utterly devoid of life, the television center continued its functions unattended. The commodore's speech had already been canned; its tape was threaded into the programmer and it would start as soon as the throb show was over.

Don watched it from a recreation lounge of the liner along with a hundred-odd other civilians. All eyes were on a big television tank set in the end of the compartment. A monitoring beam, jury-rigged for the purpose, brought the cast from Circum-Terra to the *Nautilus* and the radio watch in the ship was passing it on throughout the ship so that the passengers and crew might see and hear it.

As the day's serial episode closed, Celeste Kallikak had been arrested for suspected husband murder, Buddy Kallikak was still in the hospital and not expected to live, Father Kallikak was still missing, and Maw Kallikak was herself suspected of cheating on ration stamps—but she was facing it all bravely, serene in her knowledge that only the good die young. After the usual commercial plug ("The Only Soap with Guaranteed Vitamin Content for greater Vitacity!!") the tank faded into Steve Brodie's trademark, a rocket trail condensing into his features while a voice boomed, "Steve Brodie, with tomorrow's news *TODAY!*"

It cut suddenly, the tank went empty and a voice said, "We interrupt this broadcast to bring you a special news flash." The tank filled again, this time with the features of Commodore Higgins.

His face lacked the synthetic smile obligatory for all who speak in public telecast; his manner and voice were grim. "I am High Commodore Higgins, commanding Task Force Emancipation of the High Guard, Venus Republic. The High Guard has seized Earth's satellite station Circum-Terra. We now have all of Earth's cities utterly at our mercy."

He paused to let it sink in. Don thought it over and did not like the thought. Everybody knew that Circum-Terra carried enough A-bomb rockets to smear any force or combination of forces that could be raised to oppose the Federation. The exact number of rocket bombs carried was a military secret, variously estimated between two hundred and a thousand. A rumor had spread through the civilians in the *Nautilus* that the High Guard had found seven hundred and thirty-two bombs ready to go, with component parts for many more, plus enough deuterium and tritium to make up about a dozen Hell bombs.

Whether the rumor was true or not, Circum-Terra certainly held enough bombs to turn the Terran Federation into a radioactive abattoir. No doubt with so much under ground many inhabitants of cities would survive, but any city, once bombed, would have to be abandoned; the military effect would be the same. And many would die. How many? Forty millions? Fifty millions? Don did not know.

The commodore went on, "Mercifully we stay our hand. Earth's cities will not be bombed. The free citizens of Venus Republic have no wish to slaughter their cousins still on Terra. Our only purpose is to establish our own independence, to manage our own affairs, to throw off the crushing yoke of absentee ownership and of taxation without representation which has bled us poor.

"In so doing, in so taking our stand as free men, we call on all oppressed and impoverished nations everywhere to follow our lead, accept our help. Look up into the sky! Swimming there above you is the very station from which I now address you. The fat and stupid rulers of the Federation have made of Circum-Terra an overseer's whip. The threat of this military base in the sky has protected their empire from the just wrath of their victims for more than five score years.

"We now crush it.

"In a matter of minutes this scandal in the clean skies, this pistol pointed at the heads of men everywhere on your planet, will cease to exist. Step out of doors, watch the sky. Watch a new sun blaze briefly and know that its light is the light of Liberty inviting all Earth to free itself.

"Subject peoples of Earth, we free men of the free Republic of Venus salute you with that sign!"

The commodore continued to sit and gaze steadily into the eyes of each of his colossal audience while the heart-lifting beat of *Morning Star of Hope* followed his words. Don did not recognize the anthem of the new nation; he could not help but feel its surging promise.

Suddenly the tank went dead and at the same instant

there was a flash of light so intense that it leaked through the shuttered ports and tormented the optic nerve. Don was still shaking his head from it when over the ship's announcing system came the call: "Safe to unshutter!"

A petty officer stationed at the compartment's view port was already cranking the metal shield out of the way; Don crowded in and looked.

A second sun blazed white and swelled visibly as he watched. What on Earth would have been—so many terrible times *had been*—a climbing mushroom cloud was here in open space a perfect geometrical sphere, growing unbelievably. It swelled still larger, dropping from limelight white to silvery violet, became blotched with purple, red and flame. And still it grew, until it blanked out Earth beyond it.

At the time it was transformed into a radioactive cosmic cloud Circum-Terra had been passing over, or opposite, the North Atlantic; the swollen incandescent cloud was visible to most of the habitable portions of the globe, a burning symbol in the sky.

VII

Detour

IMMEDIATELY after the destruction of Circum-Terra the ship's warning signal howled and loudspeakers bellowed, ordering all hands to acceleration stations. The *Nautilus* blasted away, shaping her orbit for the weary trip to Venus. When she was up to speed and spin had been placed on her to permit sure footing the control room secured from blast stations. Don unstrapped and hurried to the radio room. Twice he had to argue to get past sentries.

He found the door open; everyone inside seemed busy and paid him no attention. He hesitated, then stepped inside. A long hand reached out and grabbed him by the scruff. "Hey! Where the deuce do you think you're going?"

Don answered humbly, "I just want to send a message."

"You do, eh? What do you think of that, Charlie?" His captor appealed to a soldier who was bending over a rig.

The second soldier pushed one earphone up. "Looks like a saba-*toor*. Probably an A-bomb in each pocket."

An officer wandered out of an inner room. "What goes on here?"

"Sneaked in, sir. Says he wants to send a message."

The officer looked Don up and down. "Sorry. No can do. Radio silence. No traffic outgoing."

"But," Don answered desperately, "I've just *got* to." Quickly he explained his predicament. "I've got to let them know where I am, sir."

The officer shook his head. "We couldn't raise Mars even if we were not in radio silence."

"No, sir, but you could beam Luna, for relay to Mars."

"Yes, I suppose we could—but we won't. See here, young fellow, I'm sorry about your troubles but there is no possibility, simply none at all, that the commanding officer will permit silence to be broken for any reason, even one much more important than yours. The safety of the ship comes first."

Don thought about it. "I suppose so," he agreed forlornly.

"However, I wouldn't worry too much. Your parents will find out where you are."

"Huh? I don't see how. They think I'm headed for Mars."

"No, they don't—or won't shortly. There is no secret now about what has happened; the whole system knows it. They can find out that you got as far as Circum-Terra; they can find out that the *Glory Road* did not fetch you back. By elimination, you must be on your way to Venus. I imagine that they are querying Interplanet about you right now."

The officer turned away and said, "Wilkins, paint a sign for the door saying, 'Radio Silence—No Messages Accepted.' We don't want every civilian in the ship barging in here trying to send greetings to Aunt Hattie."

Don bunked in a third-class compartment with three dozen men and a few boys. Some passengers who had paid for better accommodations complained. Don himself had had first-class passage booked—for the *Valkyrie* and Mars— but he was glad that he had not been silly enough to object when he saw the disgruntled returning with their tails between their legs. First-class accommodations, up forward, were occupied by the High Guard.

His couch was comfortable enough and a space voyage, dull under any circumstances, is less dull in the noise and gossip of a bunkroom than it is in the quiet of a first-class stateroom. During the first week out the senior surgeon announced that any who wished could avail themselves of cold-sleep. Within a day or two the bunkroom was half deserted, the missing passengers having been drugged and chilled and stowed in sleep tanks aft, there to dream away the long weeks ahead.

Don did not take cold-sleep. He listened to a bunkroom discussion, full of half facts, as to whether or not cold-sleep counted against a man's lifetime. "Look at it this way," one passenger pontificated. "You've got so long to live—right? It's built into your genes; barring accidents, you live just that long. But when they put you in the freezer, your body slows down. Your clock stops, so to speak. That time doesn't count against you. If you had eighty years coming to you, now you've got eighty years plus three months, or whatever. So I'm taking it."

"You couldn't be wronger," he was answered. "More wrong, I mean. What you've done is chop three months right out of your life. Not for me!"

"You're crazy. I'm taking it."

"Suit yourself. And another thing—" The passenger who opposed it leaned forward and spoke confidentially, so that only the entire bunkroom could hear. "They say that the boys with the bars up front question you while you are going under. You know why? Because the Commodore thinks that *spies* slipped aboard at Circum-Terra."

Don did not care which one was right. He was too much alive to relish deliberately "dying" for a time simply to save the boredom of a long trip. But the last comment startled him. Spies? Was it possible that the I.B.I. had agents right under the noses of the High Guard? Yet the I.B.I. was supposed to be able to slip in anywhere. He looked around at his fellow passengers, wondering which one might be traveling under a false identity.

He put it out of his mind—at least the I.B.I. was no longer interested in *him*.

Had Don not known that he was in the *Nautilus* headed for Venus he might well have imagined himself in the *Valkyrie* headed for Mars. The ships were of the same class and one piece of empty space looks like another. The Sun grew daily a little larger rather than smaller—but one does not look directly at the Sun, not even from Mars. The ship's routine followed the same Greenwich day kept by any liner in space; breakfast came sharp on the bell; the ship's position was announced each "noon"; the lights were dimmed at "night."

Even the presence of soldiers in the ship was not conspicuous. They kept to their own quarters forward and civilians were not allowed there except on business. The ship was forty-two days out before Don again had any reason to go forward—to get a cut finger dressed in sick bay. On his way aft he felt a hand on his shoulder and turned.

He recognized Sergeant McMasters. The sergeant was wearing the star of a master-at-arms, a ship's policeman. "What are you doing," he demanded, "skulking around here?"

Don held up his damaged digit. "I wasn't skulking; I was getting this attended to."

McMasters looked at it. "Mashed your finger, eh? Well, you're in the wrong passageway. This leads to the bomb room, not to passengers' quarters. Say, I've seen you before, haven't I?"

"Sure."

"I remember. You're the lad who thought he was going to Mars."

"I'm still going to Mars."

"So? You seem to favor the long way around—by about a hundred million miles. Speaking of the long way around, you haven't explained why I find you headed toward the bomb room."

Don felt himself getting red. "I don't know where the

bomb room is. If I'm in the wrong passage, show me the right one."

"Come with me." The sergeant led him down two decks where the spin of the ship made them slightly heavier and conducted Don into an office. "Sit down. The duty officer will be along."

Don remained standing. "I don't want to see the duty officer. I want to go back to my bunkroom."

"Sit down, I said. I remember your case. Maybe you were just turned around but could be you took the wrong turn on purpose."

Don swallowed his annoyance and sat. "No offense," said McMasters. "How about a slug of solvent?" He went to a coffee warmer and poured two cups.

Don hesitated, then accepted one. It was the Venerian bean, black and bitter and very strong. Don found himself beginning to like McMasters. The sergeant sipped his, grimaced, then said, "You must be born lucky. You ought to be a corpse by now."

"Huh?"

"You were scheduled to go back in the *Glory Road*, weren't you? Well?"

"I don't track you."

"Didn't the news filter aft? The *Glory* didn't make it."

"Huh? Crashed?"

"Hardly! The Federation groundhogs got jumpy and blasted her out of the sky. Couldn't raise her and figured she was booby-trapped, I guess. Anyhow they blasted her."

"Oh——"

"Which is why I say you were born lucky, seeing as how you were supposed to go back in her."

"But I wasn't. I'm headed for Mars."

McMasters stared at him, then laughed. "Boy, have you got a one-track mind! You're as bad as a 'move-over.' "

"Maybe so, but I'm still going to Mars."

The sergeant put down his cup. "Why don't you wise up? This war is going to last maybe ten or fifteen years. Chances are there won't be a scheduled ship to Mars in that whole time."

"Well . . . I'll make it, somehow. But why do you figure it will last so long?"

McMasters stopped to light up. "Studied any history?"

"Some."

"Remember how the American colonies got loose from England? They piddled along for eight years, fighting just now and then—yet England was so strong that she should have been able to lick the colonies any weekend. Why didn't she?"

Don did not know. "Well," McMasters answered, "you may not be a student of history, but Commodore Higgins is. He planned this strike. Ask him about any rebellion that ever happened; he'll tell you why it succeeded, or why it failed. England didn't lick the colonies because she was up to her ears in bigger wars elsewhere. The American rebellion was just a 'police action'—not important. But she couldn't give proper attention to it; after a while it got to be just too expensive and too much trouble, so England gave up and recognized their independence."

"You figure this the same way?"

"Yes—because Commodore Higgins gave it a shove in the right direction. Figured on form, the Venus Republic can't win against the Federation. Mind you, I'm just as patriotic as the next—but I can face facts. Venus hasn't a fraction of the population of the Federation, nor one per cent of its wealth. Venus *can't* win—unless the Federation is too busy to fight. Which it is, or will be soon."

Don thought about it. "I guess I'm stupid."

"Didn't you grasp the significance of blowing up Circum-Terra? In one raid the Commodore had Earth absolutely helpless. He could have bombed any or all of Terra's cities. But what good would that have done? It would simply have gotten the whole globe sore at us. As it is, we've got two-thirds of the peoples of Earth cheering for us. Not only cheering but feeling frisky and ready to rebel themselves, now that Circum-Terra isn't sitting up there in the sky, ready to launch bombs at the first sign of unrest. It will take the Federation years to pacify the associate nations—if ever. Oh, the Commodore is a sly one!" McMasters glanced up. " 'Tenshun!" he called out and got to his feet.